TANGLED PROMISE

SINFUL TRUTHS BOOK 4

ELLA MILES

FREE BOOKS

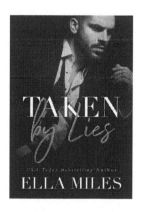

Read **Taken by Lies** for **FREE**! And sign up to get my latest releases, updates, and more goodies here→EllaMiles.com/freebooks

Follow me on **BookBub** to get notified of my new releases and recommendations here→Follow on BookBub Here

Join **Ella's Bellas FB group** to get **Pretend I'm Yours** for FREE→Join Ella's Bellas Here

TRUTH OR LIES WORLD

TRUTH OR LIES SERIES:

Taken by Lies #1
Betrayed by Truths #2
Trapped by Lies #3
Stolen by Truths #4
Possessed by Lies #5
Consumed by Truths #6

SINFUL TRUTHS SERIES:

Sinful Truth #1
Twisted Vow #2
Reckless Fall #3
Tangled Promise #4
Fallen Love #5
Broken Anchor #6

PROLOGUE

ZEKE

PROMISES ARE MEANT to be broken.

Not to me—I don't break promises.

Ever.

I keep my word.

I'm loyal, honest, and keep my promises—no matter what. It's all I have: my vows, my truth, my devotion. I may be a criminal in most people's eyes. I've watched hundreds of men take their last breaths at my hands, slitting their throats, or firing a bullet between their eyes.

I've tortured men. I've stolen, cheated, murdered.

But my one redeeming quality is that I don't break my promises. When I make a vow to someone, I keep it. I'm loyal. Enzo Black, my boss and best friend, has never had to question my loyalties; I've always given him everything. Langston, Liesel, and Kai, all of my friends, never had to wonder if they should trust me or not. They just did because I never gave them a reason not to.

They are my family. I don't get more loyal than with family. They aren't my blood, but it doesn't matter. Each of them would take a bullet for me, and I would for them.

I'm good at making sacrifices. I've stayed away from them for so long, trying to protect them. But one mistake changed everything. One moment of weakness brought my friends back into my world. One choice changed the future of my family.

I've never been one to regret things, but I regret this. I regret it. I'm not going to be able to keep all of my promises.

I've made three crucial promises in my life.

Three.

All made in love. The woman I loved as a best friend, the woman I loved as a sister, and the woman I loved as everything.

My best friend.

My sister.

And my everything.

Three promises to three strong, beautiful, powerful women.

I thought I could keep them all. I thought I had good reasons to keep all of my promises.

I never thought I'd have to choose. There was no way to know these three women would cross paths. No way to know these women would not just intersect, but their fates would become tangled with one another. No way to know the danger I put them all in by making a promise to each of them.

I can't choose between the three most important women in my life. Even if I could put one above the other, it's going to kill me to break my promises. I can only choose one. I can only keep one woman in my life forever.

When I choose whose promise to keep, that woman is the only one who will stay in my life. The others will hate me. Or end up dead.

Save one.

Destroy the rest.

An impossible choice, but a choice I'm stuck with.

This is why I don't let women into my life. This is why I want simple, uncomplicated days. This is why I'm better as the muscle, the brute, the security force in a team of people. I can protect anyone when it's just me and my muscle and my gun.

But no amount of muscle, weapons, or trickery is going to get me out of this situation.

I'm fucked.

Three pairs of eyes stare back at me, deep into my soul, begging to be the one I choose—the promise I keep.

Choose.

Choose which of these incredible women gets to live. Choose which die.

I could no sooner choose a favorite testicle.

My heart is shattered. My heart is broken in three. No matter who 1 choose, I'm only keeping one tiny part of my heart. That's not enough to sustain me. It's not enough to give to the woman I save.

Choose.

Break two of my promises.

Choose the woman who remains in my life. Choose the woman who lives.

1
SIREN

"Do you love him?" Bishop, the man who owns me, asks.

Owns—he can think he owns me all he wants, but no man owns me.

Bishop's eyes pierce mine as I stand barefoot, in jeans and T-shirt, in his kitchen. If anyone walked in on us, they would think we are just having a domestic conversation—not that he thinks of me as his prisoner and I think of him as scum that I'm about to wipe from this earth.

"Who?" I ask as I stare out the window to the garden out back that is too beautiful to be owned by a man like him.

"Doesn't matter who, you know who he is, do you love him?"

I pull out a knife from the stack on the counter and throw it at him. It hits the cabinet behind him.

He doesn't flinch. This man has experienced pain. He knows when I'm aiming to kill or just threatening. He's a lot like me in that way.

"Just because you own me, doesn't mean I'll answer your questions," I say.

"I don't own you," he says.

"Oh, really? Then what was the contract you signed with Hugo? What about the chains, the dungeon I sleep in, the other women?"

"Those are all physical. Sure, for now, I own your body. But that's not what I want."

I frown. "What do you want?"

"To own you. Someday, I'll truly own you. When you go to sleep at night, and I'm there. When you fuck your man, and I'm there. When you close your eyes, and I'm there. That's when I'll own you. When you can think of nothing else but me. When you can think of nothing but my words ringing in your ear. When you only see me in the darkness. When you do exactly as I say, that's when you are mine."

I shake my head. "You'll be waiting a long time."

"Why? Because you are already owned by another man?" He smirks.

"Julian Reed, perhaps?"

My eyes widen. *How does he know about Julian?*

"Or perhaps your lover? Are you owned by him?"

"I'm owned by no man."

He shakes his head. "I thought you couldn't lie."

"I can't."

"That sounds an awful lot like a lie, Siren."

"It's not," I say, my throat tightening. I grab another knife and fling it, this time brushing the edge of his ear, causing the tiniest bit of blood.

Bishop still doesn't move. The pain is nothing.

"You know, Siren, I've been in love before."

Why is he telling me this?

I still, waiting for the trap he's setting. With men like Bishop, there is always a trap waiting to be sprung.

"Love is the ultimate prize. It's what everyone wants. Some claim they want money, fame, power. It's all lies. All any person wants is to love and be loved."

Who knew the man is a sap?

"What happened to the woman you loved?" I ask. *Did she die?* I hate Bishop, but I don't want anyone to die because of their association with him. She probably didn't even love him. *How could a woman love a man like Bishop?*

"She stopped loving me," he says with pain in his eyes. His blue eyes have become clouds of gray and black. If he had any tears to shed, he would, but I can tell he's long past tears. It wouldn't matter that I'm here as his slave. He would cry. He would mourn his loss in front of me without shame. He just has nothing left to get out. No emotions left except for an empty, hollow shell.

His eyes glaze over for a minute as he thinks about the woman he loves. And then he snaps back to me.

"Do you love him?" he asks again.

I suck in a breath. *Does it matter if I do? What is it going to hurt telling this man?* He's a kindred spirit. He knows what loving someone who doesn't love you back does to a person. He can be my enemy and still understand how I feel.

"Yes," I breathe, and it's the truest word I've ever spoken. *Yes, I love Zeke.* I will always love Zeke until my dying breath, which, if Bishop has his way, will be sooner than later.

Bishop nods, already knowing it to be true.

"Then save him," he says.

I frown, not understanding. "I already did."

He shakes his head. "No, all you did was bring him to the fire. Right now, he's standing on the edge, just breathing in fumes. One tiny push will launch him into the heart of the flames, and once he's there, there is no going back. He'll be engulfed."

I have no idea what Bishop is talking about.

"He's not in any danger. I made sure of that."

Bishop grits his teeth. "He's loved by you—a siren. There is nothing more dangerous than being loved by you."

———

Present Day

Bishop's words ring in my ear. *There is nothing more dangerous than being loved by you.*

The words that followed are burned into my brain forever.

You're owned.

By a dangerous, ruthless, broken man.

Bishop is a man who has loved and lost. There is nothing more dangerous than a man who has lost everything. A man who has nothing to live for except to numb his pain—except for maybe a woman who has lost everything. That woman may be the most dangerous of all.

I stand in the entry of Zeke's house. Staring at the door that I forced Zeke out of with one word—Lucy.

He loves her. He doesn't love me.

He loves the mysterious woman at the ball. He doesn't love me.

Even if he does—he had to leave. He can't be with me. Bishop's words are true. If Zeke stays, he'll die, because of me.

Zeke had to leave, and I need to fix everything before he comes back. Zeke will come back. He always keeps his promises, even to evil men like Julian Reed.

Right now, I can't think about any of that. Right now, I can't even breathe.

I sob.

Tears fall hard and fast in streams over my red cheeks. If tears could burn, these would.

I feel myself shaking. My legs tremble, barely holding me up. My arms shake, and my heart breaks having just watched Zeke walk away from me. Watched him choose another woman. Watched him leave because I told him to.

He didn't fight. He hardly questioned why. He just left.

It's for the best.

Tell that to my broken heart.

My heart thumps slowly, then quickly, two thumps, then one, then three in quick succession. It no longer knows how to beat. Something so simple, something my body never had to think about, has become complicated. It can't beat anymore. It's too hard.

I wouldn't be surprised if I keel over dead. Slowly, I fall to my knees as my legs collapse.

I can't breathe, my chest constricts around my lungs, purposefully trying to suffocate me to stop the pain. My throat tightens, and air can barely make its way through the tears pouring down my cheeks over my nose and mouth.

My body wants to die. *Maybe I'll have a heart attack? Maybe this will be the end?* Dying alone of heartbreak.

My heart skips a beat, as if to say not today. *Today, I don't die. Everything I'm doing is for love.*

I'm strong.

I'm a fighter.

I won't give up.

Not like this.

Just because I can't be with the one I love doesn't mean my love ends. It doesn't mean my life is no longer worth living. I may never love again as I love Zeke, but I can love him from afar. I can protect him by keeping him away from me.

Someday, if I'm lucky, maybe I'll be able to love someone, and they can love me back without fear of danger. Maybe I won't be a siren anymore. Maybe I won't be dangerous to every person I love.

Maybe I'll go back to just being Aria Torres. *Do I want to be Aria, when Zeke calls me Siren? When I've always been Siren to him? When the name I hear falling from Zeke's lips is always Siren?*

I hear footsteps coming up the drive.

Zeke?

My tears dry up immediately. My heart beats regularly again, if not faster than usual. I stand, my legs stronger than they've ever been.

He came back.

He's not gone.

If he came back, that means he loves me. He doesn't care about our fucked up past. He doesn't care about the risk. Our love can conquer all. *Right?*

I hold my breath, knowing that I'm dreaming a little too much if I really think that is going to happen. I listen more carefully. The footsteps are too light to be Zeke. *He's not coming back, stupid heart, why don't you listen to me? You're the one who got us into this mess. I was just fine on my own until you got involved. I didn't need to love.*

The door opens—Nora.

"What are you doing here?" I ask.

She sighs. "Just a feeling that my best friend needed me."

I frown. "You're a terrible liar."

Nora walks over to me and holds open her arms.

I just shake my head. I can't be hugged by her. Not because of the lie I told Zeke. Bishop didn't ruin touch for me. Bishop ruined love for me.

I can't be touched because if she hugs me, I'll fall apart again.

"What are you doing here?" I ask, again.

Nora drops her arms. "I'm here to get you drunk."

"How did you know I needed you?"

I follow Nora into Zeke's kitchen, where she is already pouring us both drinks. "I can't say."

"Zeke?"

Nora blinks rapidly. *Yes—Zeke texted her.* I don't know whether to feel touched or angry or emotional or what. Zeke didn't care enough to fight, to stay, to figure out why I pushed him away. But he cared enough to call Nora and tell her to come, that I needed her.

"I don't need a babysitter," I say.

Nora laughs. "Good, because I'm a terrible babysitter. Can you imagine me with kids? Eww, all that slobber and poopy diapers, no thank you."

*Kids...*I imagine little babies walking around, babies with long dark hair, a sturdy frame, and Zeke's rare smile. My heart clenches. Even if Zeke came back, I could never have kids with him. There is no way to bring kids into this world. It would be a death sentence for all of us.

"Oh, beautiful. I'm so sorry," Nora says, and this time, she doesn't ask permission. She hugs me, pulling me tight to her chest. I let her.

I'm expecting to fall apart in her arms. Instead, I feel

stronger, absorbing some of Nora's strength through the hug.

Strength I immediately need as there is another knock at the door.

Zeke!

Zeke wouldn't knock. This is his own home. But that fact doesn't stop my heart from pitter-pattering, hoping it's him.

Nora looks at me as she continues to hold me in her arms.

She sighs at the expression on my face.

"It's not him," she says before even going to the door.

"I know," I whisper back. But I don't know. I'm full of hope for even a one percent chance that Zeke is behind that door.

Please, please, please.

As much as I want Zeke to stay, I need him gone to protect him. *Unless...*

Nope, he has to go. That's what's safest.

Nora walks me to the door, most likely because she doesn't think I can stand on my own. She's right; I can't. Or at least, I don't want to.

I hate that a man controls my emotions. That I'm this hurt by a man. I'm strong and independent, just like Nora. And yet, it still crushes me knowing that might have been the last time I ever spoke with Zeke in person. He could go to Lucy and then back to his old life and never return. It would be up to me to keep Julian and the rest of the danger from coming after him.

Nora opens the door with a murderous glare, prepared to destroy whoever is on the other side for interrupting her taking care of me.

Julian.

Fuck.

He grins at me. "Have a moment to talk, Aria?"

"No, she doesn't have a moment. She's been through hell these last few days. Something you don't give a shit about. You should have tried to rescue her or stop it from happening!" Nora yells at him.

Julian's eyes flitter to me as he takes in my broken appearance for the first time. Other than making sure I can still hold a gun and seduce men for him, he doesn't care.

"I did," Julian says, shocking us both.

"No, Zeke rescued me," I say.

"And I helped him. How do you think Zeke found out where Hugo was?" Julian asked.

At the mention of Hugo, my stomach coils. The first man I loved, my husband for years, the man who sold me. Now he's dead, and I'm torn because Hugo was also a man I loved. He was a broken man who needed help. As much as he deserved to die for what he did, it still hurts.

Zeke killed Hugo. He never told me, but I know he was the one who pulled the trigger, not Julian, Zeke. And I'm thankful for it.

"It doesn't redeem you for everything else you've done, you bastard. Get out! Aria needs to heal," Nora starts pushing Julian off the front step.

"Wait," I say.

Nora's head swivels to mine.

Julian breathes.

"You really helped Zeke?" I ask.

Julian pulls down his shirt, revealing a bullet hole in his shoulder. "The asshole shot me for helping him."

The beginning of a smile pulls at the corner of my mouth. It's not a real smile. A real smile will take ages. I don't even know if I can smile, but it warms me to know that Zeke shot Julian.

"Come in," I say.

Nora frowns but steps back so Julian can enter. We all walk to the living room. Nora and I sit on the couch, and Julian rests in a chair next to us.

Julian and I both stare at Nora—telling her to leave.

She crosses her arms over her chest. "I'm not leaving. I'm involved in this world now. I may not have skills like Aria or be able to shoot a gun, but I do know she's my best friend, and my role is to keep her sane and protect her. I'm staying."

I raise my eyebrow at Julian, waiting for him to challenge her. He doesn't. No man does.

And then the other corner of my mouth lifts. I can heal. I can get past this. I can smile again. Maybe not today or next month, but sooner than I think.

I feel the stab of my heart, reminding me that even when I smile again, it won't take away my pain. Nothing will.

"What do you want, Julian?" Nora asks, clearly impatient.

"I wanted to check on Aria. And Zeke—"

"He's gone," I say.

"Oh? And where did he go to? That wasn't part of our arrangement. Zeke is supposed to stay here until our deal is over," Julian says.

I shake my head. "You don't care about Zeke. Not really. You want me. You want your power. Your money. You don't need Zeke."

Julian shakes his head. "You have a week to get him back on this island and ready to complete his third task."

"Not going to happen. I want to renegotiate."

Julian laughs. "You have nothing left to negotiate with." He stands. "One week, Aria. Remember our deal."

Like I could forget.

"I'll get him back," I say, telling another lie. I have no intention of getting Zeke back here. If I was finally able to drive him away, then good. He'll be safe. I'll steer Julian's attention elsewhere, no matter the cost to me. I just want Zeke safe.

Julian nods and leaves. He still doesn't know I'm capable of lying. The longer I keep that fact a secret, the better. It means I have a power I've never had before.

When the door shuts, Nora turns to me. "What was that about?"

I shake my head and then curl up on the couch. "Just the same old bullshit. Julian thinks he can make me do whatever he wants."

"But your deal is over, right? Hugo is dead. He has no power over you anymore."

I nod. *Another lie.* Julian holds all the power, and he knows it.

Nora strokes my hair. "Come on, let's get you into bed."

"I'm not sleeping in Zeke's bed. We should go to your place."

"Nope, we are sleeping in Zeke's big ass bed." Nora helps me up, and I don't fight her. I'm exhausted from keeping track of all the dangerous men in my life.

Nora helps me strip off my clothes and slip into one of Zeke's T-shirts and sweatpants.

"Are you purposefully trying to torture me?" I ask through tears as I breathe in his scent.

Nora strokes my hair. "No, I'm helping you."

She pushes me into the bed. I have no idea how she's helping me. This seems like the opposite of moving on.

I close my eyes, feeling the pull of darkness. Zeke is gone. He didn't come back. He's gone. The pain is deep. It makes me toss, turn, and writhe.

Bishop...his eyes, his voice, his words—they push out the pain. Bishop owns me now. I don't know if I'm thankful he took away my pain or scared that the most dangerous man yet owns my dreams.

2

ZEKE

I STEP into the darkness of my bedroom.

The room is completely black, not even the light from the moonlight shines in through the slits on the blinds.

As long as I don't make a sound, no one will know I'm here if that's what I want. I haven't made up my mind. I don't know what to do with Siren. I don't know how to get her to trust me. To share the truth with me. To stop keeping her damn secrets and trying to protect me. I'm a grown-ass man with plenty of deadly skills and am completely capable of protecting myself.

Siren hurts me while trying to protect me. All it does is make our relationship more complicated. Somehow, I still end up staying. Trying to figure out the truth. Trying to find a way I can love her. Loving her and earning her love in return could be the greatest thing I've ever experienced.

So here I am, standing in the shadows of my own bedroom as I watch Siren and Nora sleep in my bed.

Nora has her arm draped over Siren's waist. Siren doesn't move. For a woman who claims she can't be touched, she doesn't seem to have a problem with Nora holding her. *Maybe it's just my touch she has a problem with?*

And for a woman who says she hates me because she thinks I sold women, when I didn't, she doesn't seem to have a big enough problem with me to not sleep in my bed.

I step closer to Siren's side to really see her.

I suck in a breath at the sight. Even in the darkness, I can see the wet spot on the front of her shirt. Her cheeks and eyes are swollen and red. She's been crying. It doesn't take a genius to know she's been crying over me.

Because she thinks I'm a monster who sold women? Or because I left?

Only she can answer that.

Siren moves, and I freeze. I'm not sure I'm ready to face her right now. I just "left" today. I don't know if just a few hours is long enough for me to figure her out. To decide what I want to do. What move to make next.

Siren isn't going to wake up, though. She's thrashing; she's murmuring; she's shaking. She's lost in a nightmare. One that Bishop most likely caused. I don't know who Bishop is, but I'm going to destroy him. I'm going to make him pay in so many more ways than the money he made me pay. I'm going to make him suffer with everything he has.

Nora, on the other hand, wakes up and looks at me with disappointment in her eyes.

"Don't look at me like that," I whisper.

She raises an eyebrow. "Look at you like what? Like I'm annoyed you are playing games with Siren. You didn't really leave, and you're having me play spy. You see that Siren is in pain and aren't immediately wrapping your arms around her. You should be lucky all I'm doing is looking at you like this."

I swallow down the guilt. This is nothing compared to

what Siren has done. *Right?* I'm just doing this to learn the truth—to protect Siren.

"Don't," Nora says.

My eyes bore into hers. "Is she alright?"

Nora strokes Siren's cheek, tucking her hair behind her ear. "What do you think?"

"I think we are both so fucked up. There is no way we can ever be together."

Nora shakes her head. "Then you don't deserve her. Siren needs a fighter. She's had to fight her entire life. If you aren't willing to fight through the walls she puts up to protect both of you, then leave for real. And don't come back. We can deal with Julian and make sure he doesn't come after you and your friends. But if you love her, then stay and fight."

Nora's right, but staying scares the shit out of me. Not because I'm afraid of a fight. I've been jonesing for a good fight. I'm scared of having real feelings for Siren. She didn't believe me before when I told her I loved her. Or she didn't care. Or she hates me because she thinks I sold women. I can't tell with her anymore. And if I tell her my feelings again, and get rejected again, I don't know if I'll be able to handle it.

It doesn't matter if you say them, you already feel them. *You love her.*

Nora's face lightens as she realizes my truth. "Follow your heart, Zeke." She strokes Siren's hair one more time and kisses her on the cheek, something I'm dying to do. "Be careful with her. Whatever Bishop did, it might have been her breaking point. She needs you to heal her. To show her love is worth it. She's been burned too many times." Nora stands.

"And what if I've been burned too?"

Nora touches my shoulder. "Then you let her heal you too."

Nora isn't careful as she walks out of the bedroom, shutting the door a little too loudly, almost like she wants Siren to wake up and find me here. *But what do I want?*

Siren is tossing more now, the pull of whatever Bishop did to her stronger. She's fighting it. Trying to push the dreams out of her head. Suddenly, she stills as if she's given up.

No! Fight dammit! I need you to fight! Stop giving up on us.

I step closer, trying to decide what to do. *Wake her or disappear?* That's my choice. I can learn more about her if I disappear and follow her actions as I did today. I can learn what she doesn't want me to know.

Or I can wake her, earn her trust, and get her to tell me the truth. I can remind her I lov—

"Zeke," she cries out. Her eyes are still closed. She's still in the nightmare, but she's fighting now.

Choose. Now.

"Zeke," she breathes out again, and my body makes my choice for her. I cradle her in my arms.

"I've got you, baby, I've got you. You're safe. It's just a dream," I say soothingly into her ear as I hold her against my chest and stroke her face. I want her to wake up from the nightmare, but I don't want it to be traumatic if I can avoid it.

Her eyes flutter open, and she smiles up at me. It's the clearest moment I've had with her. This is what I want. To make her smile. A real, genuine smile only I can put on her face. I bring her comfort and protect her. I keep her safe, and I make her come alive. That's why she's smiling. That's what I want to keep doing—making her smile, making her happy. My heart warms, watching her smile, and I can't help my own grin from spreading across the depths of my cheeks.

The moment lasts only a second. For one second, we are both happy with each other. We forget the truths. We forget the lies. The secrets. The betrayals. We forget all of it. And in this moment we just are. We love without speaking because I'm here, holding her. My touch is like fire to her, choosing her over protecting another, and she's letting me, despite thinking I'm a monster.

But moments are never meant to last.

In one blink, everything floods back into her brain, and she jumps back in the bed out of my arms.

I don't move; I stay seated on the edge of the bed.

"Zeke?" she asks cautiously, like I could be anyone else.

"It's me."

Her eyes widen as she looks around the room, trying to make sense of what's happening.

"What are you doing here?" she asks.

"What do you think?" I say, neither of us willing to say the words. Neither of us ready to say the obvious reason that I'm here—because I love her. No matter what. No matter if she hates me. No matter if Lucy is in danger. I love Siren. And I won't run away from my feelings.

"What about Lucy?" she asks.

"Don't worry about Lucy. Worry about yourself," I say with sin in my eyes and a wolfish grin. I know exactly how the rest of our night is going to go, and I can't fucking wait to push her to her limits.

3

SIREN

ALL THE FEELINGS flood over me at seeing Zeke.

Excitement.

Fear.

Lust.

Love.

The fear is strong; it's real. I'm scared for what it means that Zeke is here instead of chasing after Lucy. I'm scared for what it means to Zeke that I failed in keeping him safe. I'm most scared for what it means for my heart. I can't handle another heartbreak.

But the love at seeing Zeke again...that love is stronger than all of the other feelings combined. I have to do everything to fight it, to not to fling myself at Zeke. To keep from hugging, kissing, and fucking.

"You came back," I say, carefully, my mind still in the terrible nightmare I was having before Zeke brought me out of it.

"I never left," Zeke answers.

You could have fooled me. It sure felt like you left, at least to me.

"What does that mean?"

"It means I've been here. I didn't go after Lucy myself; I sent someone to check on her. I chose to stay."

He chose to stay. He chose to lie. He chose to spy on me. To try and figure out the truth of what I wasn't saying.

I'm fuming, but I'm also in awe. Zeke learned a lot from my manipulative ways.

What truths did he learn? Was Nora in on it? Did he bug the house? Did he hear Julian and I's conversation?

It doesn't matter because he's here.

He may not have said he's here because he loves me like he did before, but he chose me, he's here. I don't have to keep fighting alone.

Yes, you do, Bishop's voice haunts me.

I squeeze my eyes shut, trying to block him out.

"What did he do to you?" Zeke asks, his voice pained.

He drops his head in defeat when I don't answer. I'll keep the truth until my dying breath. The truth would destroy Zeke. Abso-fucking-lutely destroy him.

It destroyed me. I will never be the same. I will never believe the good in people again. I will never trust. I shouldn't even trust Zeke or Nora, but my heart belonged to both of them long before Bishop. Those connections were hard for him to sever, but he did. He destroyed my hope for any future relationships. He destroyed my ability to fully trust—even Zeke.

"Let's play our game, Siren."

Yes.

No.

I can't.

"Okay," is what comes out of my mouth.

I don't have to ask what game—our sin or truth game.

"This time will be a little different, though," Zeke says,

standing over me, a looming, determined wall of muscle. He ties his hair back, and I swallow hard to keep the drool in my mouth.

"How so?"

"We won't just play one round. We will play as many as it takes."

"It takes to do what?"

"To break you."

"Why would you want to break me?" I ask, pain burning around my heart. He didn't come back to save me; he came back to hurt me.

"Because the only way to heal you is to break you completely. Remove the hold Bishop has on you."

How does he know?

Zeke's eyes look at me with everything—pain, fear, love. He knows this is the only way to help me truly. It pains him to hurt me, even in the name of healing me.

I nod, silently agreeing. I will do anything to get rid of the torture I feel. To be free of Bishop. To think clearly instead of what Bishop wants me to think.

"You don't get to ask me any questions. You don't get to commit any sins."

I frown, not liking this at all.

"What do I get out of this?"

"Besides healing?" he asks, thinking that's good enough.

"You can't heal me. What do I get when you fail?"

"My truth. The one truth you've been dying to know. Not because Julian wants answers, but because you do." Zeke is stone as he speaks to me. He's serious. He's resolved.

Lucy. He'll tell me about Lucy. *Do I want to know the truth about her? Do I want to know who she is? Do I want to know what she means to him? Do I want to hear about his past, or current, love for her?*

Yes.

I need to know.

I'll do anything to know. If he still loves her, maybe it will stop me from needing him, from risking everything for him.

I don't have to verbally tell Zeke my answer. He already knows.

Zeke stands still, but his eyes circle the room, the wheels turning in his head as he tries to determine how he is going to break me—heal me.

He can't. I know what Bishop has done to me, Zeke doesn't.

Zeke thinks I can't stand to be touched by Zeke—it's not the truth. Zeke isn't safe around me; he needs to go away. I already failed at that, and my heart is too weak to try again.

"Can't stand to be touched by me?" Zeke asks.

I nod my lie. I can stand it. I want it. But it hurts, it fucking hurts.

No one else's touch hurts as much as his. No one else's touch feels as good either.

Zeke narrows his eyes. *Can he tell I'm lying?*

He nods, though. *So I guess not.*

Zeke cracks his neck and hands, preparing for what he's about to do. He's trying to intimidate me, but nothing intimidates me more than his love. The possibility that he really loves me scares the shit out of me. He admitted to loving me before, but it wasn't enough. His 'I love you' wasn't strong enough for me to believe because he left. His love scares me. Everything else is just physical pain. Or psychological. Not emotional. The emotions are what I can't handle.

"Do you think I sold the women? Truth or sin," Zeke asks.

I open my mouth to answer, but Zeke cuts me off. "Tell

me the truth Siren, if you choose truth. If you lie, there will be consequences."

"Death, that was our original agreement. Are you going to kill me, Zeke?" I taunt, knowing he won't.

His eyes darken, his face turns gray. "No, but I won't tell you my truth."

I stare him down. He knows, or at least, he suspects I've lied to him before. I need Zeke's truth. I can't risk it now, but I also can't risk him knowing the truth.

Zeke is going to push me with each question to choose sin. He's going to push me to my limits; he's going to make me want to answer him to get him to stop.

Bring it on.

"Sin," I say. He can't know the truth—that I don't think he sold the women into sexual slavery.

Zeke silently walks toward me. I'm still sitting at the top of the bed on the pillows, leaning back against the headboard.

I watch as he pulls a knife from his pocket and extends it.

I suck in a breath. *Is he really going to start with pain?* He thinks that is how he's going to break me. *Does he realize the kind of pain I've been through?* He's going to need to bring me to the edge of death to have a shot at breaking me. I've been there before, and that didn't even do it.

Pity lives in my eyes for what I'm sure is going to be a feeble attempt at hurting me. Zeke can't hurt me. Not really.

He doesn't speak. He grabs the hem of my shirt, pulls it away from my body, careful not to touch me, and slices the knife through the material up to my neck.

"Stand," he commands.

I take a deep breath and do as he says. The shirt falls from my body, leaving my upper body exposed.

Instead of sliding my sweatpants down my body like a normal person, Zeke inserts the knife in my waistband, pulls the material from my body, and thrusts the knife down, shredding my pants until they fall to the floor. Until I'm naked and exposed in front of him.

"That's all you got?" I ask, goading him a little.

His heated stare is his response. It chills me until I visibly shiver.

God, I want his hands on me. His lips. I want him to undress. I want to feel him inside me. I want—

"Next question," Zeke says, pointing toward the bed.

I sit back down, wordlessly.

"Do you think I'm a monster?"

No.

Again, I can't answer.

"Sin," I say.

Zeke walks to his closet and returns with silk ties.

"I didn't realize you owned any ties," I say.

"There's a lot you don't know about me, Siren. Just like there is a lot I don't know about you. But I'm about to find out a whole lot."

He holds out the tie. "Wrists."

I hold out my wrists together, obeying him, making his job easier. He carefully ties my wrists together, being so gentle and calm. Not once does he touch me, even when I squirm a little, hoping that it will force his fingers to brush against my skin.

When my wrists are tied together, he jerks them over my head until I fall back on the center of his bed. Then he ties me to the headboard.

He gathers two more ties and secures each around one of my ankles, spreading my legs wide as he ties them to the bedposts.

Nothing about how he ties me ensures that I stay put. He's just putting me in a position where he seemingly has more control, more power. Where I can't touch him, and he won't touch me.

Fuck, what did I get myself into?

My body is already heated from his longing gazes. My skin is tingling with desire from being so close to Zeke but not getting the reward of connection. My nipples are already puckered for him. I could blame it on being cold in the room, but it's because of Zeke. There is no doubt the wetness leaking between my legs is because of my desire for the man.

He's done nothing.

He's barely spoken.

He hasn't touched me.

He hasn't stripped for me.

He hasn't whispered any dirty thoughts.

He's done nothing to turn me on, except that intense glare. That flicker of desire in his eyes. The control of his body. The control over me. He's got all the power. And he plans on using it against me.

He grabs another tie, and I know exactly what he's doing —shutting me off from him. Ensuring I can't see him. I can't beg him for things with my eyes. The only way this stops is with the truth, and the truth involves breaking me.

Just before the blindfold goes over my eyes, I give Zeke one last glance.

Please, please break me. You have to. You have no idea the cost of failure...

4

ZEKE

I HAVE to do this right. I have to break her. Siren's eyes told me everything. There is more at stake than just saving us. Something deeper I have to find my way to. *But what?*

I tighten the blindfold around her eyes, doing everything I can to not touch her. It's part of my plan—good thing I have the calmest, steadiest hands.

I step back with my work done. Siren is tied up naked in my bed. Every man's dream, except it's my nightmare. I don't get to fuck her. I don't get to taste her or touch her. I have to break her.

It's killing me. I have a lot of willpower, a lot of self-control, but this is taking everything I have not to touch her, kiss her, fuck her.

I clear my throat, along with the dirty thoughts of what I could do to her in this position. I try to ignore the way her nipples peak and seem to be pointed at me no matter where I move in the room. I try to ignore her soft, throaty moans before I've even touched her. I try to ignore the wetness dripping between her thighs onto my bedspread.

Focus.

"Did you know Julian is worth billions?" I ask another question I know she won't answer. I need to ask as many questions as I can, each question more tempting to answer as I torture her body. I don't plan on breaking her with pain or torture. I plan on breaking her with the one thing neither of us has ever experienced before—love.

Love is the most powerful thing between us. It's driven us both to do things out of character. To hurt one another. It's the only way to heal us.

I watch as Siren takes shallow breaths, not able to take a full breath as she lays naked before my eyes. Her body is on high alert, trying to decide her best move to get what she wants. The problem is I don't know what she wants, and neither does she. She's a confused mess. Her desires to want me, to love me, have been pushed aside for so long in an attempt to protect herself and me.

For once, I want her to stop thinking about how to save us because the more time I've spent with her, the more I realize the best way to save us both is to give in to our emotions. To try fighting together instead of keeping each other in the shadows and fighting apart.

"Siren? Tell me the truth or let me sin," I say, growing impatient with her. I'm usually strong and in control, but I only have so much patience now. Every second I have to stare at her naked body and not touch her is another second that I have to use all of my rapidly dwindling self-control.

"Sin," she says calmly. She's worked up. I know the feeling, because my cock aches in my pants. My heart is racing. My breathing is calm only because I need her to think I'm calm and unaffected. If Siren only knew what was going on inside my body—the war I'm fighting with myself.

When she says the word, I make my move. I don't have everything planned out. I don't know how many rounds this is going to take. All night if I had to guess. Siren is a stubborn, strong woman who won't allow herself to break.

What if I break first? I think as I walk calmly to the kitchen, not letting my footsteps make a sound. I'm sure Siren is straining her ears trying to figure out what I'm doing —the waiting is part of the torture.

Being out of the same room as her reduces my ache, but only minimally. The only way to get rid of my ache is to fuck her. And I doubt that is happening.

I stare down at my erection. *Sorry, buddy, you're just going to be in pain for a while.* My heart thumps, reminding me it hurts too. *Poor heart, poor cock, poor me.*

No, I'm not a victim. I'm a fighter. And I know what I want. I don't care if this takes all night, all week, or all month. I'm going to break Siren. I'm going to rid her of whatever Bishop did. Whatever Julian did. Only when there is nothing left of her can we rebuild. Only then do we have a chance at starting over together, as it always should have been.

I grab a cup and fill it with water. I chug the glass, trying to keep my cool and get the images of Siren naked out of my head. But as soon as I push them out, the thoughts of what torture Bishop must have inflicted on her overwhelm me.

Fuck.

I'm not strong enough to heal her.

Yes, you are. I see Kai Miller in my head. A woman I once helped. A woman who soon became one of my best friends. A woman I would protect with my life. A woman who embodies strength.

You can help her, just like you helped me. And when she's healed, she will give you all the strength you need to fight.

I can do this.

I fill the cup with ice and take my time walking back to the bedroom.

Siren is right where I left her, even though she could escape the ties if she wanted to. She wants me to heal her. She wants this to work as much as I do.

She doesn't speak when I enter. Her lips are pursed like she's been focusing on her breathing. Her body stills even though I see a hint of redness around her wrists telling me she most likely pulled at the ties before getting a grip on herself again.

I set the glass down on the table with a thump and watch as Siren jumps. She didn't know I was here until just now.

I smile. I like how reactive she is to me. Even without me touching her, she responds.

This is going to be fun. Or it's going to be the death of me.

Carefully, I reach into the glass and pull an ice cube out so she can't hear what I'm doing. Her head turns toward me, sensing where I am.

I put the ice cube between my lips as I climb onto the bed, careful not to touch her despite how desperate I am. Siren said she couldn't be touched. I've watched her be touched by Nora without her reacting, so she either lied or she just can't stand my touch. Either way, by the end of the night, she's going to be begging for my skin on hers.

"Zeke," she whispers, knowing I'm over her.

I give her my answer, with an ice cube to her nipple.

She gasps in delectable delight. Her nipple hardens beneath the ice cube as I move it gingerly over her nipple, teasing it. Her body arches, and I have to pull back to keep from touching with her anything but the ice cube. I push the ice cube over her other nipple, taunting it.

She expects it this time, but her body still reacts. Her skin pinks. Her nipples sharpen. Her fucking moans shoot straight to my cock. I thought it was hard before, but I've never been this hard in my life.

Her nipples taunt me, and I lose control for just a moment. I nearly bite and taste her, just before I regain my composure. It's enough for me to forget about the ice cube. It slowly slides down her stomach. She arches and writhes. I follow the cube with a heavy gaze and watch as it stops just over her clit.

I grin as I watch her toes curl.

"Zeke," she gasps again. This time my name sounds like a prayer. The begging has already started. Maybe this won't take all night like I first thought. Maybe it will be over in a matter of minutes, because Siren can't stand not to fuck me just like I can't stand not to fuck her.

I oblige both of our desires. I take the cube in my mouth again and rub it over her clit in small circles.

Her hands grab at the headboard, her toes cling to the sheets, and her hips buck into me, begging for more.

I can smell her sweet scent as I turn her on. It draws me in, making it even more difficult for me not to touch her. When the ice cube once again slips from my mouth, I come face to face with her clit. I'm tempted. *So fucking tempted.*

But my arms remind me of what I'm doing this for. I push myself backward off the bed so quickly that I stumble onto my ass on the floor.

Jesus, that was close.

"Zeke," her voice is needy and scared. She knows this can work. I can break her. And that scares her. For some ridiculous reason, she thinks pushing me away is the only way to protect me. *Not going to happen. Not again.* I'm going to get her back. Or more accurately, make her truly mine. And then I'm never letting go.

Goddammit, though, she needs to stop saying my name, or I'm going to lose it. How can one word affect me so much?

I shake it off and try to think of my next question. I need to keep this moving before I do something stupid.

"Do you still love me?" I ask.

She sucks in a breath at the same time I do. I realize I want the truth. I don't want the sin. I need a break from this. I need one moment to collect myself because I may have more muscles than any other man I know, but I'm weak when it comes to her.

Somehow, our eyes meet beneath the poorly tied blindfold over her eyes. She sees me clamoring to my feet. She sees me weak. For a moment, I think she's going to answer. I see her want to. I see her form the words. I see her come so close.

"Sin."

5

SIREN

Jesus, did I want to answer his question honestly. Yes, I still love you, you ogre.

Yes, I've always loved you.

Yes, I'll always love you because you're my damn match. You push me. You see me, really see me. You see past the bullshit. You see past the manipulation. You detected the first lie I ever told you. You knew I needed help.

You knew.

And now here Zeke is already breaking.

But the thing is, I know how strong Zeke is. I know he's stronger than this moment. In three seconds, he's going to realize it too, and that scares me. Once he realizes finishing this game is the only chance we have at being together, then any chance I have at protecting him will be gone.

I should end this. I should start telling truths. It could save him, but I'm tired of saving him and not having him.

Right now, I'm a little bit selfish. I want it all. The man of my dreams and saving him, even if it puts both of our lives in more risk. Maybe he really can get the thoughts out of my head. Maybe he really can free me of Bishop and Julian.

Being my own person would make it easier to keep us all safe, right?

I don't know. Maybe it's just my selfishness talking, but I want to believe that. I want to believe that being with Zeke is better than fighting for him on my own.

We lock eyes under the crack of my blindfold. *This is your only chance. Fight for me, for us, or lose me forever. Either way, I'm protecting you with my life.*

Honestly, I have no idea which way will ensure your protection, Zeke. But of course, I love you.

He sees my unspoken words, and like I suspected, I no longer see the fear or sense the uncertainty. He's ready to break me. There is no going back. He's going to succeed. My heart is happy, but my mind is freaking out, convinced I shouldn't let him break me. My mind screams that it's the wrong move.

But my heart is tired of listening to my brain. My heart wants to feel good for once.

Heart or brain? Which is right? Please, for once, let it be my heart.

I hiss as I feel hot wax hit my chest. It's such a stark contrast from the coolness of the ice that, at first, it completely shocks my system.

Eventually, just like the ice, the heat turns me on. It makes me wish Zeke was the one touching me, especially with my heightened senses—I want more.

But then my brain does what it does, trying to protect us all. I'm quickly brought back to Bishop.

Any man can pour wax on your body. He isn't special. He's not worth saving. Bishop's voice rings in my head.

"Don't let him win," Zeke says, sensing the battle brewing inside me.

I gasp as more wax hits my stomach.

38

"Don't let me win either," he continues.

Wax hits my nipple, and I moan at the pleasure. "What do you want, Siren? Not Julian, not Bishop, not me—you? What do you want? What does that voice in your heart say?"

That it wants you. That together, we are stronger. But I've fucked up so fucking much. Zeke can't trust me. I don't even trust me.

No one trusts you. So listen to me, Bishop's voice says.

Zeke sighs and scrapes the wax off my stomach with some plastic tool.

"Have you ever lied to me with your words?" Zeke asks next, his voice stronger, more determined.

Yes.

"Sin," I whisper.

I hear a growl and then the familiar press of a knife against my heart. He holds it in place but doesn't pierce my skin.

"I'm not afraid of you," I say.

"And why is that?"

"You won't hurt me."

And then I feel a slice. It's not deep, but it's enough to get my attention.

"I can. I will. In any relationship, whether it be friends, family, or lovers, you always end up hurting the other person even when you don't want to. You can't be afraid of me hurting you or you hurting me. We've hurt each other plenty, and we still want each other."

I can handle the pain. What about you, Zeke? You haven't been handling it well so far.

He slices me again, against my stomach just over the mark Hugo made. It hurts, knowing he did the same thing Hugo did. It causes my eyes to water, especially when he doesn't immediately bandage and heal me. He doesn't immediately apologize.

Suddenly, I feel his breath against my ear. "I fucked up. I'm sorry. I never want to harm you. If I could promise I would never hurt you, I would promise it. But it's a promise I've learned I can never keep, because I'm human. I'm not a god. But I will do everything I can to make it up to you."

He removes my blindfold. Then he lifts his own shirt and slices across his beautiful abs in the same way he did mine.

"Never again," he promises. "Never again will I hurt you with a knife. That I can promise, but I can't promise I won't hurt you in other ways."

I nod.

It's not enough.

"Do you want me to touch you?" he asks.

We are both panting. Both desperate to fill our ache, our desire. That's not what I need, though. I know what I need to be rid of Bishop. It won't happen, because no man can love a siren like me, not after what I did.

"Sin," I say stronger than ever.

He blinks away hope, like he thought he was close. He walks over to the nightstand and pulls out a vibrator. The buzzing sound makes my toes curl before he even touches me with it. But it's not what I want.

"No," I say.

"It's not up to you; you chose sin."

He presses it against my clit. I'm so sensitive that I expect to come immediately. I expect the release I don't want.

My body is stronger than I realize. It doesn't want a release from a rubber object, either. It wants Zeke.

Zeke rubs the vibrator against my body. Every nerve is

firing. I'm moaning like a maniac. My body moves, unable to decide on leaning into the vibrator or away from it.

My head is a mess, unable to decide what to do. My body is a conflicted bundle of nerves. But my heart, it's strong. Stronger than ever. It won't budge. It won't let me come. It won't let Bishop in. Not even Zeke.

Zeke made everything clear. He healed me by pushing out everything else. All the doubt. The confusion. The control.

I finally feel powerful. I feel like I can take on the world. I know exactly what I want and how to get it.

After a few minutes of me not coming, Zeke stops. He turns the vibrator off and lets it fall to the floor.

Zeke is exhausted. He's weary. He bites his lip to keep from screaming in frustration, most likely. He doesn't know the victory that just happened in my own body.

"Do you want me to fuck you?" he asks, his voice defeated.

I grin, liking his choice of question. Because this time, I'm going to answer. This time, I'm done choosing sin. I'm done saving Zeke while denying us both what we really want. There is no point in saving Zeke if I don't let us both live. If I don't trust him. If I don't love him.

"No, I don't want to fuck you, Zeke."

His eyes widen in shock.

"I want something else from you. Something I'm not sure you're willing to give. Something I don't deserve because I've been scared. I've been fighting it, trying to protect you. Not because it was the best way to protect you, but because I was scared. I'm done being scared, Zeke."

He grins. "Finally."

6

ZEKE

I DON'T KNOW what happened. I don't even know if I should believe she broke and healed. But I choose to because we need a fresh start. We need this. We need each other. I'm afraid we are both the missing pieces. Without the other, there will be no more healing.

"I love you, Siren. I love you, Aria. I love you. I'm still learning who you are. I'm still learning how to trust and earn your trust. I don't even know what loving you means. But I love you. I fell, and now I'm ready to deal with any consequences of loving you," I say.

Siren closes her eyes, and for a moment, I think I did the wrong thing. Maybe it was wrong to tell her I'm in love with her. *Did I just undo any healing progress?*

A single second later, her eyes open like fire. The next second, she's free of her bindings. Then she's coming at me like a dragon, full of fire, rage, and strength. The beautiful, magical kind of dragon you don't think exists, but then you see it with your own eyes and don't have a choice but to believe.

Siren doesn't need me. She doesn't need a man in her life, but damn, do I need her.

She stops short of me, inches from my face, neither of us touching.

"I love you too, Zeke Kane. That's how I should have responded when you told me you loved me before."

My heart breaks. *Who knew that hearing 'I love you' can damage a heart as much as her walking away from me?*

She places her hand on my aching heart. Her touch heals me.

"I'm sorry for lying. I'm sorry for so many things. I thought I was doing the right thing. I thought I was protecting us both. I'm sorry for not trusting you. I'm so sorry," she says, her eyelashes fluttering, but not in the manipulative way I've seen her behave around other men. Her eyes are fluttering because she loves me. Just like her hand is on my heart because she loves me.

I hold her hand to my chest. "I can touch you?"

"Yes, it never hurt." She winces, scared to tell me the truth. "Well, it did because I was scared. I was scared of what Bishop did to me, and I thought it was better that you got as far away from my fucked up head as possible."

"What did he do to you?" I ask, needing to know.

She blinks, her eyes blank. "This is going to sound weird, but I honestly don't know. I did, but when I pushed Bishop out of my head, it's like my memories disappeared."

I study her eyes. It's the truth. I want to know what happened, but maybe it's better this way. The pain is permanently gone from her memory.

She looks up at me with a tinge of fear.

"I love you, focus on that," I say.

She bites her lip. "Prove it."

That's all I need. We've both been torturing ourselves for

hours. I plan on making love to her and fucking her at the same time.

She yanks my pants off, and our bodies collide in more ways than one. Our lips, our hands, our stomachs lock. Our blood mixes together against each other's stomachs. My cock settles between her legs instantly.

"Don't make me wait, Zeke." Her voice is soft and needy.

I lift one of her legs and slide home.

She swallows hard at the connection that's always been between us, but now we accept as right, not wrong. We have a lot to figure out—a lot of trust issues and truths that need to be said. But for now, this is enough.

"Fuck me," she says.

"Love me," I respond as I thrust into her hard, pushing her back onto the bed. Her legs widen for me and wrap around my waist, pulling me deeper inside her, where I've always belonged.

"I hate you for making me wait for this. For torturing me and not letting me feel you inside me," she says over my lips as we taste, gnaw, and bite at each other.

"You think you had it rough? I had to stare at the most beautiful naked woman in my bed and not touch her."

She giggles. "You get to touch me now."

"Forever," I say with seriousness in my eyes.

We both stop moving as I say the word forever. It's such a big word. In some ways, it's a bigger word than love. Love can change, grow, or disappear, but forever never ends.

I don't want to take the word back. I mean it. I want forever with Siren. I can't imagine another woman in my life —only her. Our life together may still be short. People like us don't live forever. We'd be lucky to hit forty. We won't have the fairytale: the kids, the house, and the PTA meetings. We won't have a steady job or normal income or friends we meet up with on the weekends.

We could have our forever, though. We could stop the lying, the deceit, the secrets. We could promise each other to put each other first. To love each other first.

Siren's lips fall open as her eyes search mine for the truth of how I feel. To see if I'm full of crap. To see if I'm manipulating her into loving me so I can destroy her like she's destroyed me.

I let her in, past the bullshit and lies. I let her see me—the man beneath the armor I always wear.

"I'm your anchor, Siren. And you're mine. There is a reason we keep coming back together, even through the lies. We need each other. We've been going about this all wrong. We've been loners for so long. Together though—together —we would be unstoppable."

Her eyes water.

Shit, I didn't mean to make her cry. I'm so sick of hurting her. I pull out a little, but she grabs at my chest, reaches up to the base of my ponytail, and yanks me to her, my cock slamming deep inside her.

We both growl at the pleasure—pleasure we both need more of. *Why did I decide now was the time to talk?*

Because we are both vulnerable, and it has to happen.

Slowly, Siren reaches up and kisses me tenderly on the lips. It's different than her other kisses. There are no fireworks, but it doesn't mean it isn't the best damn kiss of my life. This kiss is full of promise, tenderness, and love. This kiss vows we are in this together—no matter what, we will work together as a team.

The unity gives way to a massive eruption. We can't hold back anymore, not after controlling ourselves for so long. We still have so much to discuss. So much hurt to work through. But that doesn't matter anymore. We love each other, and love can get us through anything.

I drive inside her, needing her to know how badly I need her. Her nails dig into my back, telling me she wants this as much as I do.

Her hands sneak up to my hair, and she rips the scrunchie from my hair.

I half-laugh, half-growl. "You really don't like the scrunchie, do you?"

Her eyes fall back as if she's thinking about something else. "I'm undecided about the scrunchie." She slips it onto her wrist, in the same way I saw my friend Kai wear my old scrunchie earlier. "But I know I love my beast-man."

"I thought I was your anchor?"

I thrust longer, forcing her to arch her back to take me in deeper.

"You are. But in the bedroom, you're my beast."

I grin. Then I make good on my nickname. I turn into a beast. I grab her hips, angling her up so I thrust deeper inside her. My teeth clamp onto her nipples, nibbling on the soft points, and I can feel her cascade of wetness wash over my cock as I do.

"Fuck, Zeke," Siren purrs.

How can missionary feel so good? I'm usually an ass man and prefer taking women from behind. But with Siren, it's all good. Everything. Being face to face with her, eye to eye, lip to lip, chest to chest, and cock to pussy, is my new favorite.

The face Siren makes is full of frustration, desperation, and need. I got her so worked up before and so close to orgasm, but then denied her. Her body is having a hard time letting go. Even though the sex is out of this world, she's still in her head.

"I got you, baby," I say with every emotion I feel.

"Just shut up and kiss me," she says, trying to pull my lips back to hers as I thrust again, changing the angle, and I watch with amusement as her eyes go big at the deeper penetration.

I do kiss her. I sweep my tongue inside her mouth, and her tongue battles mine right back. It's not going to be enough to get her over the edge. I know what will, though.

I slow down my thrusts to painstakingly slow, and then I brush her hair behind her ear, making sure to touch every sensitive spot on her neck as I do.

"Zeke, please," she begs me to speed up again. To make her come.

I am, beautiful. I am.

My lips hover over her ear, breathing hard, hot fire down her neck as I pull my cock out, so only the tip still rests inside her. She squirms, trying to get me back inside.

"I promise I'll love you forever, Siren."

And then I slam inside her as a gasp escapes her throat.

Her body lets go, no longer holding back. I promised her with my words; now it's time to promise her with my body. I pump into her once, twice, and then I feel it, her orgasm clenching down, pulsing around me.

"Love—Zeke," she screams. Her words not a complete sentence like mine were, but she gets her point across.

Her words alone would have made me come but combined with the thrusting, her walls pulsing around me, and the beautiful naked woman beneath me, I explode in my own orgasm.

I wish I could say I did the gentlemanly thing and cleaned us both off. But instead, I collapse on top of her, not even having the strength to pull out of her.

But I don't miss her whispers before I fall asleep.

"Forever."

Forever—a promise and a curse. A promise we both vow to keep.

I have no idea if either us are going to be able to keep our word.

7

SIREN

FOREVER.

There have been plenty of moments that completely changed my life. Decisions I made. People I met. Answers I gave.

But I suspect nothing will have as big of an impact as that single word—forever.

It's what I've wanted my entire life. To be loved by a man forever. And to love him in return forever.

Loving him isn't the problem, I realize.

Forever, is.

There is too much we both still don't know. Loyalties we have to people from our pasts. Truths we have yet to spill. I want to tell him everything. *But if I do, will he still love me?*

Probably not.

But I'll tell him everything he wants to know. EVERY-THING. I'm not going to sit for an hour and spill my guts. For one, it will take much longer than an hour to tell him everything. But if he asks, I'll tell him the truth—no more games.

Zeke will tell me his truth in return. I'm just not sure I want his whole truth yet.

We made so many promises. Promises I wish we could keep. Promises of love, of trust, of forever.

Promises that should be easy to keep. But we are human. We're flawed. The dangers we face are worse than most.

Last night, the promises came easily. *But how will Zeke feel in the morning? In the daylight, when we aren't fucking, and it's just us? Will he still want to be with me? Still want to be with the siren who has hurt him more than loved him?*

The morning light shines in my eyes, and I roll over, ready to face whatever Zeke wants. I'm hoping he's up for a round of morning sex, even though my aching, sore pussy thinks we should rest for a few days first.

The bed's empty.

What the hell?

I grab the sheets to cover my body as I sit up and search the room for Zeke. The room's empty. I listen for the sound of the shower running in the bathroom—nothing.

Shit. Was last night all a dream? I remember Nora in my bed. *Did I want Zeke in my bed so badly that I imagined everything I desperately needed? For him to love me, heal me, fuck me?*

No, no, no, no...

This can't be happening.

It had to be real.

My heart bursts. My tears fall. My face crumples in my hands as I realize it was all a dream.

I hear footsteps. Nora's most likely.

I wipe the tears, trying to hide my pain from her. I'll feel so embarrassed if she knows I had a dream last night so vivid I thought it really happened.

The door opens and...

Zeke.

He's standing in the doorway, looking hot as ever. He's shaved his face, and he has a new scrunchie tying his hair up.

Wait!

I look down at my wrist and see a red scrunchie wrapped around it. I move my legs and feel the familiar ache from a hot round of sex. I take in the softness of Zeke's eyes, and then he mischievously winks at me.

Last night wasn't a dream. It was real.

I sigh into the sheets, my heartbeat returning to normal levels.

"You okay?" he asks, no doubt noticing the redness around my eyes and dried tears on my cheeks.

I smile. "Never been better."

He looks at me suspiciously. "Siren."

"Yes?"

"We promised, no lying."

I bite my lip. "I'm not lying. I've never been better. Now five minutes ago, I was in hell thinking last night was all a dream, but then I realized it was real."

He exhales. Apparently, thinking I was already lying to him hurt him worse than I realized.

We are both so fragile right now. Both been through so much pain. We have to be careful with each other if we are both going to survive.

But then I see what's in Zeke's hands—a suitcase.

"Where are you going?" I ask.

"To see Lucy," he answers.

Anger shoots through me so fast. He was in my bed last night, promising me love and forever. This morning, he goes running off to the first love of his life.

"Siren, do you have something else you would like to ask

before you murder me?" Zeke says lightly, amused by my reaction.

That's when I spot a second suitcase. I don't pack much of anything when we've traveled before, but apparently, Zeke thinks I'm going to need clothes to travel to the ends of the earth where I've ensured Lucy is safe.

"Are you going alone?"

"No, you're coming with me."

I smile. "I am, am I? You haven't even asked."

"That's because I already know the answer."

I shake my head. "We are going to be the death of each other, aren't we?"

"Probably." He grins, and it's adorable.

I remember why he's going to see Lucy. I lied to him and told him she wasn't safe. I said she needs him. Lucy, I'm sure, isn't exactly safe. At least not by most people's standards, but she's as safe as she can be for the moment.

My anger washes away and quickly gets filled with regret. I lied to him to push him away, and now it's backfiring on me. I have to try out the new thing we promised each other. Telling the truth.

I'm terrified, that with one sentence, I'm going to destroy the promises we agreed to. That I'm going to hurt him again. That he's going to stop loving me. Everything I did, I did to protect him, save him. It's hard to explain unless you have all the facts. It could take years to explain to Zeke all the facts.

"Zeke?" I say.

"Yes?"

I let out a whoosh of a breath. There is no going back now. Just tell him.

"Lucy isn't in any new danger. At least not any more than she was."

Zeke blinks.

"I lied earlier to get you to go away because I thought it was safer for you not to be with me," I continue.

He just stands like he's waiting for a bomb to drop, but I just dropped it. I have nothing else to say.

"Zeke?"

"Yea?"

"I need you to talk to me, with words."

"Okay."

"Okay? That's not words. Plural. I lied to you. I hurt you again. I'm sorry."

"Okay."

I sigh, frustrated. "Again, that's not really telling me how you feel."

"I already knew you lied. At least, I had a good hunch. It's why I'm here and not chasing after Lucy."

I wince. *Okay, that hurt.* The only reason he stayed was because he knew I lied, not because he chose me over Lucy.

"You're upset," he says.

I nod. "A little."

"Why?"

"Nevermind." I climb out of bed, but Zeke races over, boxing me in from leaving the room. I'm naked. He's dressed. I'm vulnerable. He has his armor up. It isn't fair.

"Tell me the truth."

"I'm just hurt and jealous of your relationship with Lucy."

Zeke smiles like an idiot.

"Why are you smiling?"

"Because you're cute."

"How am I cute? I lied to you. You should be mad at me."

"I am."

"You sure don't look it."

He grins brighter. "I've already forgiven you for lying. That was a tiny lie for a good reason, compared to the other shit. Right now, I'm more amused that you are jealous of Lucy."

I fold my arms over my chest, which pushes my boobs up. He stares at them, smiling bigger. *Asshole.*

"Stop staring at my breasts."

"Why? I like your breasts and your breasts like the attention."

"Not right now, they don't. I'm mad."

He folds his arms, mimicking me. "Why are you mad?"

"Because you are being ridiculous. You should be mad, not wanting to fuck my boobs."

"Can't I be both?"

"No."

He rolls his eyes with lightness in his eyes.

"Stop trying to undress me with your eyes."

He smirks. "You're already undressed, baby. I don't have to imagine."

"I'm not your baby."

"Fine, what do you want me to call you?"

"Not baby."

"Okay, I'd really like to fuck you, not baby."

I sigh at his playfulness this morning. "You're exhausting."

He takes my hand and spins me to him, so my back is to his front. He kisses my cheek. "And you're grumpy in the morning. How did I not know that?"

"Seriously? You aren't mad?"

He lets go. "I'm mad. But I love you more. I want this to work. Sure, I could explode. We could fight. And then have awesome makeup sex. Or we can just get right to the sex and skip over the mad part."

"I can't skip it."

He shakes his head. "You can. You just don't want to."

He runs his hands down the side of my body, and I shiver.

"Lucy isn't a threat to you."

I bite my lip. "She sure feels like one."

"That's because you don't know the truth yet."

"Then tell me."

"I'd rather show you."

"Show me?"

"That's why we are going to Lucy. Not to check on her, but to keep my promise to you. To show you who she is to me."

I exhale the anger.

"I love you, Siren. I trust you. I don't want to hide my past from you. As much as I love your jealous side, I'd prefer you not kill my old friends just because you're jealous. So I'm going to fix it. Okay?"

"Okay."

"Now, I'm going to fuck you, and then we are going to get on Nora's plane, and she's going to take us to Lucy."

I shouldn't want to fuck again, not after our fuck session last night. But I'm already wet and turned on. There is no way I'm getting on a long plane ride without fucking Zeke first.

"Fuck me, Zeke."

He grins. "My pleasure, forever."

"Forever?"

"Yea, your new nickname. I think it works. I'll fuck you into next week, forever."

I smile. It's silly and cheesy and romantic. And exactly what I want.

8

ZEKE

"So...um..." I rub my neck nervously in the back of the airplane that Nora is flying us in.

Siren sits next to me with her eyes closed. "Spit it out, Zeke."

I'm trying. I really am, but I've never been in this position before. It's a little embarrassing. She will understand and be completely fine with my new situation. At least, I think she will be. I just don't exactly know what her position is either.

We may be screwed. I don't know how to fix this situation.

"Um..." I start again, but I can't say the words. I'm the type of man who handles things. If there is a problem, I don't say the problem until I've already found a solution. But I don't have a solution.

Siren rests her hand on my thigh, and she isn't helping the situation. Even when she strokes my leg in a comforting manner, all she's doing is turning me on.

I hold her hand, getting her to stop.

She looks at me, wide-eyed. "This is serious, isn't it? Whatever you're about to say?"

I nod.

She sits up, holding my hand tighter, and looking at me.

"Um…" *Goddammit, why is this so hard for me?*

"What is it?"

"Idon'thaveanymoney," my words come out in a rush all together, so there is no way for her to decipher what I just said.

She cocks her head to the side in confusion. "Can you try that again? I didn't catch a word of it."

"Yea, and speak louder, so Aria doesn't have to re-tell the story to me later," Nora shouts from the cockpit.

Siren laughs at my mortified expression.

"You're going to tell her?"

"Well, I don't know what I am or am not going to tell her yet, since you haven't actually told *me*. But yes, usually, I tell my best friend everything."

"I'm not your best friend?"

She smiles. "Am I yours?"

Yes, no. I don't know.

She shrugs. "She's my best friend. Just like you have other friends. What we have is so much more than friendship. It's better."

I nod, this conversation is so not helping my manhood.

"Tell me."

I stare at the cockpit where Nora sits. She'll find out eventually, so I might as well get this over with.

"I'm broke!" I quickly yell at the top of my lungs.

She frowns. "What do you mean? You had plenty of money last I checked. Millions, in fact, and an amazing credit score."

"You looked up my credit score?"

"Of course." She doesn't look the least bit guilty.

I shake my head. "Well, look again. It's all gone."

"Did you get robbed?"

"Not exactly."

She looks at me blankly, not understanding.

"Bishop demanded I pay him everything I had to get you back."

Her eyes are wide as I look away in embarrassment. Not because I gave up everything to get her back. I would do that time and time again, but because I have nothing to offer her. No money. No future.

Her hand touches my cheek in a comforting manner. "You think I care about your checkbook?"

My eyes meet hers and say it all. I'm the man; I'm supposed to provide for you; take care of you. I can't do that if I don't have any money.

She strokes my cheek, her eyes searching mine for why I feel this way. I'm usually secure. I know exactly who I am. But with Siren, I want to be better than who I usually am. I want to be stronger, more powerful, more manly. I want to be everything she deserves.

Her eyes soften, and I swear I see a tear in the corner of her eye. She sniffles, and the tear is gone.

"You're incredible, do you know that?" she says.

"I'm incredible because I'm broke?"

"No, you're incredible because you did what it took to get me back. You gave up everything to get me back. You valued me more than you valued money that you worked your ass off, and most likely risked your life, to earn. That's incredible."

She touches me against my cheek, and the spark hits me like a ball of fire. It hits me in the heart, and if I wasn't already hers, I would be now.

"The money was nothing compared to you. It was an easy decision."

"And it's an easy decision to love you even if you are poor and going to be poor forever, because let's face it, you don't have any skills that are going to earn you money again," she rolls her eyes, and every word is soaked in sarcasm.

I smile and then stretch my arms over my head before reclining the chair back.

"You know what? I think I'm going to enjoy this sugar momma life. You make all the money while I just look pretty and wait for you to fuck me," I say.

She hits me playfully on the chest. "Uh, uh. You are going to get a job, mister. I don't care if it's just serving fries at McDonald's, I'm not going to do all the work."

"Really? Even if me not working means I'll have more energy for this?" I whisper into her hair over her ear. I'm sure Nora could hear us if she really wanted to. I can see her out of the corner of my eye, making out half her body. Nora seems focused on flying the plane, and I'm focused on convincing Siren that I'm in this forever and getting in her pants.

My hand slips beneath the band of her jeans, and then I'm cupping her sex, providing just enough heat and pressure to drive her wild, but not enough to leave her satisfied.

"Zeke, what are you doing?" she hisses, but her voice doesn't sound angry. It sounds turned on, with a drop of need.

I tuck her hair behind her ear and brush my tongue over her earlobe. "I'm showing you how good it would be to be together forever. Whether we are both working or not. Whether we are poor or rich. Whether we are free or always on the run. It could always be like this..."

I unbutton the button on her jeans, then roll down the zipper.

Siren puts her hand over mine as she eyes Nora in the front of the plane.

"Zeke, we can't. Not here," she says.

I'm not planning on fucking her in the back of the plane. But I do want to hear her moan, pant, lose control. I do want to know that I can turn her on anywhere anytime. I want to know that I'm the only man in her life who can make her feel this intense amount of pleasure.

I dip my finger beneath her panties. "I can stop."

She curses as I touch her sweet spot, already wet, already buzzing with need.

"Yes," she manages to get out.

I stop, but I don't remove my hand. She's going to have to tell me to remove my hand.

She blinks like she can't believe I actually listened to her, that I actually stopped.

She bites her lip, debating with herself.

"Nora, how much longer until we land in Miami?"

"Thirty minutes. I need to focus on landing, so don't expect me to chat much until we land," Nora shouts back.

Siren's eyes lighten in mischievous desire, her cheeks pink, and her tongue licks her bottom lip.

"Don't stop," she whispers, knowing Nora won't be paying us any attention. Not that I care if Nora hears Siren's screams, or notices that my hand is in her best friend's pants.

I lean forward, taking her bottom lip in mine at the same time my fingers start moving in her pants again.

Her eyes roll back in her head, and a soft cry bellows from her throat.

"You're going to want to bite down on something," I say,

nibbling on her ear, then kissing my way down her throat as I dip two fingers inside her.

"I can be quiet," she says so softly I can barely hear her, proving her point.

I smirk and then rub my thumb over her clit. She squeals.

She clamps her hands over her mouth. She wasn't that loud, but she got my point. If she doesn't want Nora to hear her, she needs to bite down on something.

"Fine," she says, grabbing my face and pulling my lips to her. She chooses my bottom lip.

It's sexy and painful, and I love it when her teeth sink into my flesh. I growl. She raises her eyebrows as if to say I better be quiet or she won't be rewarding me later for what I'm about to do to her.

I laugh quietly, but then she nips at my lip again until I taste blood. We are eye to eye, mouth to mouth, finger to pussy. And I can't think of a better position I've ever been in.

I feel heat cover my lip as she groans into it, trying to keep herself as silent as possible while my fingers work. In and out of her slick entrance. Over her tight clit.

Siren trembles in my arms, her eyes are wide, her teeth sink further into my lip until I'm sure she's creating a hole in my lip. I don't care about my pain, or soon-to-be disfigured lip. It's all worth it to know how I'm driving her wild, how crazy I'm making her.

She grabs my shirt, gripping it like she's trying to hold onto a bucking bull for eight seconds. She can't decide between letting me finish, knowing the consequence will be her screaming my name, or telling me to stop and denying herself an orgasm.

I see the moment she no longer has a say. She's already hanging onto the edge of her orgasm, and even if I stopped everything, she'd still come. *It would be less intense, but what fun is that?*

I want her to scream my name. I want Nora to know, along with the people on the other end of Nora's headset. I want the world to know how I make Siren come, and I'm the only man who gets the pleasure.

Siren tries to bite down on my lip; she tries to hold it in. It's a good effort, but not one I'm going to let her win.

I squeeze her clit, intensifying everything. She gasps at the same time she screams. Then I feel her coming around my fingers. Her body shatters, her eyes roll back, and her teeth sink down back into my lip when she realizes she's supposed to be biting down on my lip, not screaming my name.

It takes her a full minute to recover enough to release my lip from her clutches. Another minute to let go of my shirt. Another minute until her breathing returns to semi-normal instead of marathon levels.

She closes her eyes and runs her hand through her hair, taking a deep breath. And then she looks at me with a bright, bashful smile.

"That was—there are no words," she says.

I put my hands behind my head, leaning back. "Good, because if I was going to lose my bottom lip, I wanted it to be worth it."

"What?" she screeches, sitting up and staring at my lip. She grabs my cheeks and turns me toward her. Her shoulders slump back into a relaxed state when she realizes I was kidding.

It doesn't stop her from playing nurse. She finds a Kleenex to clean off the blood on my lip and grabs an ice cube, wrapping it in a paper towel to hold against it.

"I'm sorry for hurting your lip," she says.

"I'm not, and you're not really sorry, either."

She grins. "I'm not. I just thought it was the right thing to say."

I shake my head. "The right thing to say is the truth, Siren. You won't hurt my feelings if you are being honest."

She nods. "I like being honest with you."

"Good, because I like everything with you."

"Five minutes till landing," Nora shouts. "Seatbelts."

Siren buttons her jeans, and we both put our seatbelts on. Nora turns her head and gives me a wink. There is no doubt she saw, or definitely heard, what we were doing.

I won't tell Siren, though. That's something the two friends can talk about if they want. I'll stay out of it. But I don't regret making Siren come. The glow of her skin and the weight off her shoulders every time I get her to relax is worth it.

"I didn't want to ask you earlier, but now that you are relaxed, what did you tell Julian? Or does he think we are both on the run?" I ask, not sure what answer I'm hoping she gives me.

I want Julian out of our lives. But I want us safe. I want to play our cards right when it comes to Julian. He has all the power, the money, and who knows what allies on his side. As much as I want to say that we are both running from him, it's not a smart move. I don't think Siren would do anything reckless without discussing it with me first.

She takes a deep breath. "I told Julian you ran."

I nod. It makes sense to make me the bad guy in this.

"I told him I was going after you. That I'd follow you and see if you led us to Enzo Black first before I got you."

She swallows, apparently not liking what she has to say next. "I told him I'd bring you back."

I nod and then stare straight ahead as we land. Siren has

to keep her promise to Julian. We need him to think that she's still loyal to him, whatever promises she has made, whatever men she's determined to keep safe. She has to keep her promise to Julian, just like I have to keep all the promises I've made.

We have to go back. We have to find a way to defeat Julian before my five rounds with him are up. I've completed two rounds. I have three left. My time for figuring out how to destroy him is limited.

Lucy has one missing piece of the puzzle. One clue as to why Julian is after Enzo Black. Although, I'm not sure if Lucy is going to agree to help me or not.

Siren stashed Lucy in Lithuania for goodness sakes. It's not exactly a fun tourist place where Lucy could enjoy her life. She's going to be pissed that I got her involved in this life again when I promised her I wouldn't.

But I promised Lucy I'd keep her safe above everything else. The same promise I made to Enzo to keep Kai safe. The same promise I made to myself to keep Siren safe.

My list of people I need to protect keeps growing, getting longer every day. It doesn't bother me, though. That's who I am. I protect. And someday, I'm going to die protecting someone I love.

I glance over at Siren, the woman I promised forever to. I just hope, for her sake, that day comes a long, long time from now.

9

SIREN

FLYING TO LITHUANIA TOOK FOREVER. Days, not hours. Especially when you fly to Lithuania by way of Antarctica.

Okay, so we didn't really fly to Antarctica first, but we might as well have. To keep Lucy safe and away from Julian, we needed to keep them from tracking us. We took every precaution. We flew under aliases. We boarded a train when we got to England and then flew out of France. We took buses. We chartered small planes under other identities.

We could have still been followed, but we did everything we could to prevent that from happening. And even with all of our precautions, Lucy will likely need to be moved again.

Zeke takes my hand as we step outside the airport in Lithuania. It's freezing cold. Both of us bought a coat, but it does nothing to prevent the chill of the wind from pulsing through us. There is a reason I prefer the tropical climate of St. Kitts to this.

Both Zeke and I are on edge, but for completely different reasons. We haven't talked about Lucy at all. About what seeing her means for her, and for us. But it's been on the forefront of our minds. When we traveled, when we fucked, when we slept in cramped motel rooms we paid for in cash so Julian couldn't find us.

Lucy was always on our minds.

Zeke, I'm sure, is thinking about ways to keep her safe. Us arriving is an oxymoron. Zeke and I are the most skilled people to protect her, but we are risking her life by being here. Julian only cares about Lucy because we do.

I want to know who Lucy is, and I'm scared she means more to Zeke than I do. I'm fucking terrified.

When I moved Lucy from Seattle, I did it from afar. I met with the team in person, ensuring they were prepared for the job. And then I spent my time traveling in the opposite direction of Lithuania, hoping Julian would follow me instead of her. I respected Zeke, and decided it was best not to meet Lucy in person until he wanted me to.

Zeke squeezes my hand as if to tell me everything is going to be okay. I try to believe him, but I can't. Not without meeting Lucy in person. Not without seeing their relationship. Not without the truth.

This is the first stop on a long list of painful truths we both have to share with the other. But it's a part of loving each other. If we can survive each other's truths, we can survive together forever.

"So this Lucy girl..." Nora starts.

Both Zeke and I glare at Nora for ruining our moment of silence. Neither of us has talked about Lucy. But of course, leave it to Nora to force the issue.

"What about her?" Zeke asks.

"Who is she exactly? I mean, I've flown around the world twice, ridden on a rocky train, and thrown up in disgusting buses. I slept in the grossest motels for this woman. I think I deserve to know who she is," Nora says, with her hands on her hips.

"You didn't have to come," I say, shooting her look to drop it.

"And miss out on all these hot Lithuanian guys? I don't think so," she says.

I frown. "We aren't here to get you laid."

"I know, but it sure would help if I have to listen to you two fuck. God, I almost sprung for a nicer hotel last night just so I could get some sleep. Motel walls are paper thin."

I roll my eyes.

Nora looks to Zeke. "So, who is Lucy?"

Zeke stills as if it is going to hurt to tell us who Lucy is.

"Is she an ex? A best friend? A sister? Your baby mama? What?"

"Yes," he says, and then hails a cab.

He lets go of my hand, grabs our suitcases, and starts lifting them into the back of the cab. I stand frozen, partially from the frigid cold, and partially from the shock of how Zeke just answered Nora.

Yes.

One fucking word. *Did he mean yes to all of them? Or yes to some of them?*

Lucy is an ex-girlfriend, a best friend, his sister, and his baby mama?

I don't know which hurts worse. My hands clench over my stomach.

The last one. The last one fucking hurts.

Lucy had his baby. *Zeke is a father?*

It's something I will never do. I will never bring a baby into this world. Not until it's safe. I'll never be a mother.

I glance over at Nora, who has the same reaction as I do. A rarity, Nora always has words.

Finally, Nora walks over to me. She puts her hands on my shoulder. "It's going to be okay."

I realize in the moment why Nora felt like she had to come. Not because of the adventure or hot guys, but because she instinctively knew I needed her here. I would need my best friend to face Lucy and Zeke's relationship.

I lean my head onto Nora's shoulder. "Thank you," I whisper, holding back my fear and tears.

She strokes my hair. "No matter what happens, we will always have each other."

I nod, even though it's not exactly true. There are plenty of things I can think about that Nora can't be there for me. I only allowed her to come because this trip isn't that dangerous; at least it's only dangerous for my heart.

When I'm faced with real danger, Nora won't be by my side. I won't let her. I won't let her be dragged down into my fate. My world. My life. Someday, I'll push her out.

We climb into the back of the cab, all three of us. Nora sits in the middle. Zeke doesn't object. He looks out the window. Nora pulls out her phone and uses Google Translate to communicate with the cab driver.

"What is Lucy's address?" she asks Zeke.

I'm the one who answers. After all, I'm the reason Lucy is here instead of France or Italy, somewhere more comfortable where I'm sure Zeke would have tried to hide her. But it wouldn't have been as safe.

She gives the cab driver Lucy's address, and then we sit in silence as the cab moves us through the city.

Finally, he stops in front of an old house that looks like it should be condemned. I wince when I see it. Whoever Lucy is to Zeke, she didn't deserve to have to live in these conditions. I was just trying to keep her safe; I wasn't trying to ruin her life. Although, I have a feeling it's going to be hard for Lucy to understand.

Nora pays the driver, and we all step out. Zeke gets the

bags, and we all stand in front of the house. A strong wind would probably knock it over.

Nora and I both stare at Zeke, waiting for him to take charge and walk to the door first, but he doesn't. He just stands, holding our bags.

"Zeke," I say quietly, hoping it's enough to break whatever spell he's under.

It doesn't.

I look at Nora, not sure what to do.

"Does she have any security guards?" Nora asks.

"Yes, but I already texted them and told them we were coming," I answer.

"So if I go knock on her door, they aren't going to shoot me?" Nora asks.

I shake my head.

Nora steps forward. I grab her hand, getting her to stop. "You don't have to..."

"I know. But you'd do the same for me," Nora answers.

I let go of her hand as she walks to Lucy's front door confidently. Not like she's about to destroy my relationship with the man I love.

Nora knocks.

I stand quietly.

Zeke continues to hold our bags.

No answer.

Nora rings the doorbell.

One second.

Two.

Three.

A million.

And then the door opens. A woman steps out. She doesn't look like I expected. I thought she'd look like an angel complete with wings and a halo. I thought I would never live up to her beauty.

And I won't, but just because we are so different.

My olive skin is beautiful, but not comparable to her light.

My long dark hair is the opposite of her blonde with blue highlights.

My skin is scared with knives; hers is marked with tattoos.

But we do share something in common—pain and love for Zeke. It's clear her life here hasn't been easy, but when she spots Zeke, everything about her body language changes. When she looks at Zeke, it's like everything she cares about returns to her.

"Zeke," Lucy breathes out, as if she's seen a ghost.

And then she is running past Nora like she didn't even know she exists.

My eyes land on Zeke, to see if he's still frozen or not. He's definitely not still frozen. He drops the bags and is running toward her. They both have a smile, but there is also something more intense behind their gazes. Something that they both recognize. Something I'm not privy to.

I watch as they move closer to each other. Five feet of distance becomes three, then one.

They both halt less than a foot apart. Close enough they could lean forward and kiss each other.

They don't kiss. They don't touch. They just stare at each other, trying to gauge what the other is thinking, and breathing each other in like two dogs trying to determine if they've met each other before.

And then...SLAP.

Lucy slaps Zeke across the cheek.

He huffs at the sudden hit but doesn't seem surprised.

When his face turns back, they both smile and laugh. Then they start on some ridiculous handshake they've obviously shared for years. The kind school kids have with each other. They've known each other for a long time.

"Don't ever ship me off to a country this cold and poor ever again," Lucy says.

And then it happens. The moment I've feared. Zeke lifts Lucy up off the ground and spins her around like she's his favorite person on the planet. She giggles, and then she grabs his cheeks and kisses him right on the lips.

I can't watch. I turn my head. She kissed him. He didn't stop her. He didn't turn away. He let her kiss him.

I meet Nora's gaze, which is soft and passionate but not angry. *Did she not see them kiss?* She should be ready to kill Zeke on my behalf right now.

"Lucy, let me introduce you to my friends," Zeke says.

Friends? Really, I'm just his friend?

I give Nora an eye roll. She gives me a 'play nice' look back. We are both walk toward Lucy and Zeke with fake smiles on our faces.

Zeke's smile is completely genuine and stretches wider than I've ever seen it. Whoever Lucy is to him, one thing is for sure: she makes him happy.

"Lucy Greene, this is Nora Taylor. She's an excellent pilot and the sassiest woman I know," Zeke says, walking Lucy over to Nora.

Nora smiles genuinely at Lucy, as she shakes her hand.

Geez, is everyone falling for this woman?

"And this is Aria Torres," Zeke says. I get no other introduction. No smart remark. Nothing to tell Lucy who I am to him.

I'm just his friend.

I hold out my hand. "I'm the reason you are in rural

Lithuania in winter instead of relaxing on a beach somewhere."

She takes my hand, gripping it tightly, all while keeping her smile firmly on her face so Zeke has no idea we've just become enemies.

"Pleasure to finally meet you, Aria. I've thought about you a lot these last few weeks," Lucy says.

"I'm sure you have." *Just like I've thought a lot about you.*

I still have no idea how Lucy fits into all of this. Except I do...I just don't want to admit it. I don't want to know Lucy is Zeke's real love of his life. I'm just a fun distraction.

"We should go inside, it's freezing out here," Lucy says.

We all smile at her, as Zeke keeps his hand at her waist, while Lucy leads us inside.

I can do this. I can do this. Lucy has been through a lot. Don't be a bitch. Zeke is just being nice to his friend and ex-lover and whatever else she is to him.

I look around carefully once inside. Her two guards are sitting in the living room watching TV.

Jayden and Dylan.

I nod at them, silently thanking them for keeping the bitch alive. Although right now, I wish they would have done a worse job.

That is until I see Zeke's eyes lighting up at some joke Lucy told him. His giggles are high-pitched, the opposite of masculine. But it's so damn sexy, how free he is right now. He's not worried about Julian, or Bishop, or even my deceit. With Lucy, he can just be himself.

I won't stand in the way of that. If Lucy is the woman for him, then so be it. I'm sure he acts this way around his friend Enzo Black. Seeing Zeke like this makes it even more clear that I need to get him back to his regular life and stop hogging him all to myself.

"What are we watching?" Nora asks, plopping down on the couch between the two brawny men.

The men stare at her. "Football," Jayden says, looking at her suspiciously like she's a spy or something.

"Excellent! I love the English team," Nora says, snatching a beer from Jayden's hand and drinking it.

Jayden blinks rapidly like he can't believe this woman, but then he smiles. Just the tiniest bit. I doubt this tough man ever smiles. Nora got him to smile in two seconds flat.

I wrap my arms across my body as I stare at Zeke and Lucy locked in a conversation about the good old days.

Lucy looks at me and flashes me a look of ownership, staking her flag on Zeke.

Fine, he's yours. You win. I just want him happy.

I try to say all of that back. I'm afraid I'm not used to this acting nice thing, and it comes out as a threat.

Lucy smirks and then tangles her hand in Zeke's hair at the base of his neck, twisting his mane around her finger just like she thinks she has Zeke twisted around her finger.

Fuck. I can't do this. I know Zeke wanted to bring me here to tell me the truth about who Lucy is to him, but I can't stand to find out she's the love of his life or was. Or is his baby mama.

"We need to talk, privately," Zeke says, his eyes cutting to mine for the smallest of seconds, letting me know I'm not invited to this private meeting.

"Of course, babe," Lucy says, taking his hand and purposefully interlocking their fingers.

Don't look. Don't watch. But I can't tear my eyes away from them as Lucy drags Zeke down the hallway to a bedroom —*her bedroom.*

I feel like I'm about to cry, but I also want to storm down the hallway and break the door down to demand answers. If

Zeke doesn't want to be with me, if this whole time he's been playing games, then I deserve to know the truth. Instead, I'm left in the dark.

"Come here, babe," Nora says, using the same nickname Lucy used for Zeke.

"Don't call me 'babe' ever again," I say as I walk over to Nora, who is holding her hands out like she wants me to sit on her lap. So I do.

"Move over, boys, give us room," Nora says as she cradles me in her lap.

Instead of moving away, though, the two men move closer. Dylan puts my feet in his lap as he rubs my legs gently. Jayden strokes my hair.

My eyes widen. "Guys, what are you doing? This isn't in the job description. You are supposed to protect Lucy, not me."

Dylan shrugs. "You hired us to protect Lucy. And Lucy is not the one who's hurting right now. She has her protection. But you, you need us."

I glance up at Nora, who I know is the real reason these two men are comforting me. Nora wants them to, and they both want in Nora's pants. If they play their cards right, they will both end up in her bed tonight, probably at the same time.

"Thanks," I say, loving a moment of attention.

"Always, babe," Nora says with a smirk.

I'm going to kill you, I whisper back.

10

ZEKE

"WHAT THE HELL WAS THAT?" I ask as soon as I close the door carefully behind me, ensuring Siren doesn't realize I'm pissed as fuck at Lucy.

Lucy sits on the edge of her bed, crossing her legs so her skirt rises up dangerously high on her thigh.

"Don't play games with me, Lucy. I know you better than anyone."

She tsks. "No, you used to know me better than anyone when we were kids, teenagers, not now. Now, you don't know me at all."

"I know you aren't a heartless bitch. I know you were trying to goad Siren into thinking our relationship is still something it isn't with that kiss."

"Siren?" Lucy raises her eyebrows.

"I mean, Aria." I run my hand through my hair, still not understanding why I introduced Siren as Aria to Lucy. The only possibility is that I want to keep Siren to myself.

"Siren is some nickname? I'm guessing she really fucked you up if that is what you call her," Lucy says, her voice soft.

I don't answer. I don't need to explain to Lucy what Siren

means to me. What we've been through. What we will go through. Lucy isn't privy to every piece of my life anymore.

She sighs then pats the bed next to her. "Sit."

I do.

We both sit in comfortable silence. Like it's been days since we've seen each other instead of years.

"You doing okay?" I ask.

"As well as I can be," Lucy answers.

"Can you really believe it's been ten years?"

Lucy snorts. "Yes, you look like an old man. I think I even see a gray hair." She plucks at my hair, and I fight her off.

"I don't have any gray hairs."

"And you've really let yourself go. Geez, where is the scrawny boy I used to know?" She punches the muscles in my arms.

"I've never been small."

"Nope, you weren't."

"And what happened to the sweet, high school cheerleader? Now you have tattoos and blue streaks in your hair?"

She shrugs.

"It fits you," I say.

"Thanks, it does, doesn't it?"

I nod.

She lets out a loud breath. "What am I doing here, Zeke? I get a call from Aria, Siren, whoever she is, saying I have to go. To pack one bag and head to the airport. Bodyguards would take me to safety. What the hell? And why the hell weren't you the one who called me?"

"I failed," I say, letting the weight of my words hit me.

I look at Lucy. "I failed. I'm so sorry."

She frowns. "I guessed that."

"A man named Julian Reed is looking for you. I don't

think he realizes who you are or what you have yet. But I owe him a debt, and so does Siren. He threatened you to keep me in check, not because he knows who you are."

Lucy's eyes go big. "I guess it was bound to catch up with me eventually. I just hoped it would happen when I was in my eighties and had lived a long and happy life."

"I'm not going to let anything happen to you, Lucy."

She shakes her head. "You can't promise me that."

"I promised I would protect your secret. And I've kept my word all this time."

She stands up, pacing, as if she's just now realizing the danger she's in.

I stand up and grab her shoulders, looking into her eyes. "I promise. I won't let Julian or any other man hurt you. They won't find out your secret; I won't let them."

She doesn't blink, so neither do I. We are locked in a staring contest, both trying to let the other know how badly we need these promises to be true.

"Why are you here, Zeke?" she asks, her voice so quiet I'm not even sure she said anything.

"What?"

"You heard me. Why are you here? You aren't here because you want to promise to continue to protect me like you always have. Why are you here?"

I drop my arms, preparing to cover my jewels before Lucy knees me in the balls. "Siren. I'm here because I need you to talk to Siren."

Lucy laughs. "I should have known it was for pussy."

"Siren isn't pussy. She's..."

"She's what? Your girlfriend, fiancée, wife? Don't kid yourself, Zeke. Whatever she is, this is all she'll ever be. She'll never be your serious girlfriend, and definitely never your wife."

"Why not? I could be a great husband."

Lucy shakes her head. "You could be, if you changed everything about your life. You can't be a good husband, not when you would give your life to protect your boss and his friends. You can't be a bodyguard and a husband. You can only be one or the other. You can't protect others while vowing to put your wife first. You have to choose. And you already know you will choose as you always have: a life of protecting others."

"What if I'm tired of protecting others?" I ask.

She looks at me with sadness. "I shouldn't have made it seem like you have a choice. You don't. It's in your DNA. If put in a situation where you had to choose between saving yourself so you could return home to your wife and kids or protecting Enzo Black, it wouldn't even be a choice. You would save Enzo every time, even if it meant certain death. That's who you are. You can fight it, but in the end, it's your destiny."

She touches my cheek like that is somehow going to take away some of my pain. "It's why I had to let you go."

Our eyes meet. It's only a partial truth. The real reason she let me go is much more complicated. But I don't call her out on it.

"Will you talk to Siren?" I ask, ignoring the intensity of our conversation. I don't believe Lucy's words are true. There has to be a way I can be a good husband someday while still protecting my boss and my friends. There has to be. I just haven't figured it out yet. In the meantime, I need Siren to trust me. Lucy is the biggest area of distrust.

I can tell Siren about my past, but it would mean more coming from Lucy.

"She doesn't trust me," Lucy says.

I raise my eyebrows. "I wonder why."

Lucy shrugs like how she behaved earlier was completely innocent instead of marking her territory on me. A territory Lucy no longer gets claim to.

"It's really good to see you again, Luce. I never thought I'd get the privilege."

"I feel the same," she smiles.

I walk to the door. "She doesn't trust me either, and it hurts." I open the door, knowing just how to play Lucy to get her to help me. I just put the final nail in.

"Okay," Lucy says.

I smile, not looking back.

"I'll do it," Lucy says.

I turn to give her a curt nod and then head out to the living room to deal with Siren and Nora. I have a feeling I'm about to walk into a lion's den. Both women are going to be pissed, and rightly so.

I needed to talk to Lucy first to get her on my side again and to reprimand her for the kiss like I'm hers. Now that that's handled, I have to deal with the consequences. I just hope I barely fractured Siren's heart instead of stabbing it.

But when I see Siren curled up on the couch, snoring in Nora's arms, two large men stroking her, and Nora's glare up at me, I know I've really fucked up. A simple apology won't work.

11

SIREN

I KEEP my eyes closed to hold in the tears and pain. The longer I keep my eyes closed, the longer I can pretend Zeke is still mine. I can pretend that we still have a relationship. That he didn't bring me here to destroy me by showing me how much he still loves Lucy.

I can pretend all of this isn't real.

But I can't stay this way forever. I'm not a coward. If Zeke doesn't love me, doesn't want me, it's time to face that.

Nora scratches my back as if to agree—it's time.

So like a flipped light switch, I open my eyes.

The living room is small. The room only has a couch and a TV sitting on a box, not even a TV stand, not another chair.

There are four of us on the couch. Dylan, Jayden, Nora, and I. But none of them is who I see when I open my eyes.

I see Zeke Kane leaning against the doorframe staring at me with regret in his eyes.

Well, too bad. You should have thought about how it would feel before you let that bitch kiss and touch you. *Of course, I'd be pissed.*

His eyes search mine for forgiveness. I can forgive. I've done plenty of bad shit. But not here, not like this, not in front of everyone. My pride is too hurt.

I sit up, half sitting on Nora's lap and half on Dylan's.

Zeke's jaw ticks as he sees where Dylan's hand is rubbing on my back, dipping low, almost touching my ass on each downward stroke. He's jealous, just like I was. That has to be a good sign.

"I'll make you coffee," Zeke says, staring at me.

Coffee. In the past, he's been able to make things better by bringing me coffee. I could use some caffeine. My body is sore and groggy after my little nap. I stare at the TV. The soccer game is still tied one to one. I didn't sleep for that long; I'm just tired. I guess watching the man you love fall back in love with his ex will do that to you.

Zeke walks into the tiny kitchen. There's just a coffee pot, microwave, and single cabinet.

He starts fidgeting with the coffee maker, cursing up a storm when he can't get the thing to turn on.

Jayden snickers, obviously aware of how to fix it. But now he's on team Nora, which includes team Siren. So he won't be helping him.

"It's broken," Lucy says, now leaning against the door-frame where Zeke was a moment ago.

"I'll go get you some coffee then," Zeke says, ready to run out into the freezing cold to get me coffee. To do anything to keep me from giving him dirty looks like I'm currently flashing him.

"No," Lucy says.

The room stills, like a chilly sheet of ice just covered us all, forcing us to freeze. That's the effect Lucy has on a room.

"It's really not a problem. I'll be gone ten minutes," Zeke says.

Lucy shakes her head. "You don't know where the good coffee shop is."

"Okay, so tell me," Zeke answers.

"Siren and I can go get it. We need to chat anyway," Lucy says, staring me down, daring me to say no. And it's Siren now, not Aria. Zeke must have slipped up and told her what he calls me.

I look at Nora, begging her to come with me.

"Nope, I'm not coming. This is a nail-biter. I don't want to miss the end of the game," Nora says.

I frown at her. *Some friend she is.*

I stand up, deciding it's best if Lucy and I just go alone. There's a good chance only one of us will be returning, and if I was a betting person, I'd bet on me.

Zeke senses it. "Maybe I should go, too."

Lucy grins. "Nope, girl talk. It would bore you." Then she flashes Zeke a look, clearly confident that she can take me.

I smirk. So cocky. She has no idea what I'm capable of.

"At least take Dylan or Jayden with you," Zeke says.

Lucy laughs. "I think they'd both rather stay and protect Nora. You might want to hire me new bodyguards because I'm pretty sure they will follow Nora when you leave."

"Hey, you can't blame us for falling for the hot, sassy woman. Like Siren would let us go anyway," Dylan says.

"Still, I'd feel better if one of them does their damn jobs and goes with you," Zeke says.

Lucy rests her hand on Zeke's chest, while flashing me a grin and a look from the corner of her eye. She knows exactly what she's doing.

"Siren is more than capable of protecting me. I bet she knows how to use a gun better than either of my guards do," Lucy says.

She's right. I do.

I raise my eyebrows and cross my arms, waiting for Zeke to give me permission to take Lucy out on my own. Lucy looks like a strong woman, but from what I can see, she's never held a gun in her life.

"Fine," Zeke says with a pout.

"Good boy," Lucy says before walking to the tiny closet to grab her coat. She's still wearing a damn skirt even though it's a million below. She slips on some fury boots—like that's going to help her.

"Don't hurt her," Zeke says, grabbing my arm as I go to grab my coat.

I roll my eyes to wash off the sting of pain from him thinking I'd hurt her. And he didn't threaten Lucy not to hurt me.

"Don't worry, I'll bring her back in one piece. I wouldn't dare threaten your precious Lucy." I pull my arm free, grab my coat, and rush outside before even putting it on. As soon as the wind and snow hit me, I realize that was a mistake.

———

I follow Lucy into the supposed best coffee shop in town. The smell that hits me when I first step inside instantly curls my stomach. There is no way I'm going to be able to drink anything from a place that smells like this.

"It smells retched in here," I say, scrunching my nose.

"Yep, welcome to Lithuania. If you wanted good coffee, you should have left me in Seattle."

I wince. I didn't even think when I was sending her here about the lack of good coffee. Coffee probably meant a lot to her working in the industry in Seattle. I was just trying to keep her safe, but good luck convincing Lucy of that fact.

There are exactly three tables in the coffee shop. They're all made of mix-matched furniture, with giant holes in the upholstery and bugs crawling around the feet. Lucy doesn't seem surprised or bothered at all as she walks up to the counter, greets the man in Lithuanian, and then orders a drink. Her pronunciation is a little choppy, but for only being here a few weeks, she's picked up the language well.

She turns to me, daring me to ask for her help with ordering. She doesn't know my past, though. She doesn't know that I've spoken English, Spanish, and French since I was born. I traveled with my parents when I was young on missionary trips. Language is as easy as breathing to me. Even if I don't know a language very well, I pick it up fast by just listening to others. It's the one thing I feel like I'm a fast learner at.

"Labas," I greet the man behind the counter.

"Labas," he huffs back.

I place my order in Lithuanian. "I'd like a coffee, black. Actually, some sweetener would be nice," deciding that whatever disgusting coffee he's about to serve me is going to need something to sweeten it up in order to drink it.

Lucy looks at me with raised eyebrows. "You grew up here? Is that why you sent me here?"

I shake my head.

She frowns and then rolls her eyes as she realizes I'm just good with foreign languages. "It was a good call on the sweetener. You won't be able to drink the sludge without it."

We both wait at the counter for our coffees and then take a seat at the table by the window, which I instantly realize is a bad choice as the window isn't very insulated. We both have to leave our coats on to stay warm.

I wince when I taste the coffee.

"You don't get to complain about the coffee. You are the one who dumped me in this hell hole," Lucy says full of fire.

"How about a thank you for saving your life?" I snap back.

"I wasn't really in that much danger. If I was, Zeke would have run to my side immediately. So forgive me for not thanking you for ruining my perfect life and sending me here to this frigid hell."

"I was just trying to protect you. But if you'd rather die, be my guest."

Lucy shakes her head. "Zeke hasn't even told you why you're protecting me, has he?"

I tap my fingers on the outside of the coffee cup, trying to keep my hands warm, while also trying to decide how to answer.

"No, he hasn't," I answer truthfully. Lying still sucks too much energy out of me.

Lucy studies me closely. "You really can't lie?"

"I haven't been able to lie for years. I've only recently learned how to, but it's very rare that I can. And I've only ever been able to lie to—"

"Zeke," Lucy finishes for me.

I nod.

"Do you love him?" she asks.

"Do you?"

"I asked you first. Whether I love him or not is irrelevant," she says.

"Why?"

She shakes her head.

"Why are we talking?" I ask, avoiding answering her question.

"Zeke thought we should."

"Why?"

"Because he wants you to know the truth, and he doesn't think you'll believe the truth coming from him."

I nod, realizing that as much as I hate Lucy, I do trust her to tell me the truth. Even the parts that Zeke might have tried to sugarcoat for me.

"Then tell me what you brought me here to tell me. Then I can figure out how to get you some better coffee."

Lucy chuckles. "You promise? Even after what I'm going to tell you?"

"Yes, I promise to get you better coffee, no matter what you tell me."

"I'm sorry," Lucy starts.

I frown, and my eyes squint, trying to understand how her story is starting by apologizing to me.

She laughs at my reaction. "I meant the story starts with an apology."

I grip my coffee cup harder. Lucy is going to be the death of me. I can feel it.

Lucy's eyes roll back as she remembers how she and Zeke met. "'I'm sorry'—those were the first words Zeke ever said to me. He apologized for stepping on my foot. Even at five years old, he was large compared to me. It hurt, but then I saw the sweetness in his eyes, and the pain melted away."

This hurts. The sweet childhood memories. What I would have given to have a best friend like Zeke growing up.

"Zeke wrapped his large arm around my scrawny shoulders, and he told me that he would protect me. That was the promise that changed everything. If I would have known what he was going to have to protect me from over the years, maybe I wouldn't have let him make that promise."

I bite my lip, begging Lucy to continue. I need to hear what he means to her. Or, more importantly, what she means to him. It's more than a childhood friendship and a silly promise—so much more.

"For a long time, we were friends. I was his shadow, and he was my man of steel. He protected me from bullies, from older girls, even from my parents."

I nod, understanding how close you can feel to someone who protects you. It's why I felt so connected to Hugo for so long.

"We were best friends. And then we became like step-siblings. When I had no food, Zeke would feed me. When I had nowhere to stay, I would sleep in his bed. He protected me. But I wasn't part of his world. I wasn't part of his friend group. As we got older, he would stop hanging out with me publicly. He would only protect me with threats to the others in my class, but never with his physical protection. He said that was to protect me too. He wouldn't allow me to get messed up in the dangerous life of working for Enzo Black. I was better than that. I was destined for greater things. That's what he always told me."

Lucy takes a sip of her coffee, unaffected by the bitter grounds that I can see floating in her cup.

Please tell me this is where their story stops. They were friends who later became like siblings. I can live with that. But Lucy keeps talking.

"Senior year, everything changed. Zeke was one of the big men on campus. He never played sports. He didn't want to risk getting hurt. That would have taken him away from protecting his precious Enzo Black. But he didn't need sports to be popular. He didn't need a letterman jacket for the women to swoon and throw themselves at him.

"He dated most of our class, except me. I thought it was because he thought of me as a sister, not a girlfriend. But one drunken night when I crawled into his bed, feelings were spilled. I love you's exchanged. We didn't fuck that night. Just kissed. We both wanted to be completely sober when we crossed that final step. But it was a magical night. One of the best nights of my life..."

Fuck. No, I can't keep listening. Why would Zeke do this to me? Why would he bring me here to hurt me like this? I can't handle hearing how much they loved each other. How much they meant to each other. I can't handle hearing she was the love of his life, and I'm just getting in the way now.

Lucy stops talking as she notices my reaction. She's a strong woman who knows exactly what she's doing. She knows how to slice through my heart as easily as Zeke does, and she would have no problem inflicting the first wound.

She doesn't comfort me. She doesn't rush the story she wants to tell to explain that they were all wrong for each other. That their story ended in pain and hatred. She doesn't reassure me in any way. She just watches me like I'm an experiment she's running. If she says certain words, she wants to see if I'll react the way she expects.

I don't want to show weakness in front of this woman. I never show weakness. But I can't hide my tightened chest, my burning face, and flush hot skin. I shed my coat and fan myself with my hand, trying to take deep breaths.

One, two, three.

Finally, I'm calm enough to listen to the rest of her story. "I want to hear the rest." My voice is pathetic and weak. The complete opposite of who I am. I guess I'm weak for Zeke.

"The best night came the following night, when Zeke got us a hotel room overlooking the ocean and fucked my brains out."

Yep, those words hurt. I already guessed that they'd fucked, but hearing her say it, hearing her say they were in love, that she was Zeke's first love—there is nothing that could prepare me for this.

I down the cup of coffee, just to have something else for my senses to focus on. The bitterness, the sharp taste of the sludge, the erosiveness of the coffee on my teeth and throat.

Lucy smiles with her eyes—*the bitch.*

"Can you handle more?"

"Yes," I hiss back, reminding myself that caring for a man I love is not weakness. It's strength. I love Zeke Kane. I love him, and there is nothing Lucy can say that will change that. I just don't know if Zeke will love me back when this conversation is over.

"We fucked like bunnies for months. In Zeke's bed, his car, the janitor's closet at school, the beach—"

"I get it; you fucked a lot."

"It was the best spring and summer of my life. I finally found someone who understood me, who loved me, who cared about me."

Zeke is a good man. I don't know how this story ends. I don't know how they dissolve their relationship, or if today is the day they pick it back up. But I know that Zeke is a good man, a great man, in a relationship. He's a giver, a protector, always worrying about the person he's with.

"And then...it happened," Lucy says.

I close my eyes, preparing my heart. "What happened?" I ask, opening my eyes, needing to see the truth.

"I got pregnant," Lucy says.

Turns out, Lucy doesn't need a knife. She doesn't need a gun to shatter my heart. Just three little words.

She got pregnant.

She had Zeke's baby.

It's incredible that Zeke has a child. Something that is part of him. Something I can never give him. My world is too dangerous to bring a child into, but what I wouldn't give to have the option. To be able to have a family with Zeke.

Lucy watches me, my every movement. The torture, the pain, the heartbreak. Not only can I not win, but I shouldn't if there is a child involved. I shouldn't interfere if they love each other. I should give them a chance to be a family.

Damn.

I want to be selfish, truly selfish. I want to take Zeke and run. I want to prove to Lucy that he loves me more than her. That I win.

But I can never win.

"More?" she asks.

I suck in a breath and then nod. I'm not sure I can handle more. I don't want to hear about the happy birth of their baby. I don't want to hear about what tore Zeke away, and why he's back.

But I don't have a choice. I have to know.

"I lost it..."

I was staring down at the table, feeling completely sorry for myself, until I hear Lucy speak. I don't have to look at her to know her eyes are filled with tears, her throat has tightened, and pain has spread through her body.

When I finally look at her, I see it all on her face. The pain I felt earlier was nothing compared to the torment I see on Lucy's face now.

I take her hand instinctively, forgetting all about myself, just needing to comfort a woman who has lost something it's clear she desperately wanted.

Lucy lets me take her hand. For a moment, we sit in her pain. There are no words that can bring her comfort. Nothing can ease the pain she felt all those years ago.

"I'm so sorry," I finally say.

"Thank you," she says.

I squeeze her hand but don't let go. Whatever else she has to tell me, she needs to know I'm on her side. I won't let my own pain and cattiness hurt her any more than she's already been hurt.

"When I lost the baby, I wasn't sure if I was relieved or broken. Zeke would have made a great father. He would have protected that baby with his life. But we were still babies ourselves, barely nineteen. Zeke had a career ahead of him with Enzo's company. And I...well, I realized as much as I loved Zeke, he wasn't mine."

Her words heal me. *Zeke isn't Lucy's. But is he truly mine?*

"We both took the news hard, not sure really how to feel. We both felt like we lost a bit of ourselves. Slowly, the fucking reduced until we were no longer fucking. The calls stopped. The texting became only the bare minimum. Until we no longer knew what each other was doing. Until we didn't really know each other anymore. Until we both became each other's secrets.

"Sure, we would smile when we saw each other. The hugs Zeke gave me were some of the best. But we were never the same. The loss made us realize that."

I nod.

But that doesn't mean they stopped loving each other. It doesn't mean that now that they are older, and have lived a part, they won't want to start a relationship up again.

"More?" she asks.

Fuck, there's more. I can't handle more. My heart is hurting for Lucy, for Zeke, for myself.

I need to hear whatever else she has to say. I look her in the eye, telling her to finish, but that I can't handle much more.

"I thought Zeke was out of my life for good. I thought he was only going to be the odd stranger that if we ever ran into each other at the supermarket, we'd laugh and say how we should catch up. I didn't think we'd be a big part of each other's lives ever again."

Shit.

"I needed a protector. I was in trouble. And I knew only Zeke could help me. And he did. He protected me. He saved me. He promised me. And he's kept my secret for years."

I stiffen. "What secret?"

"I can't tell you my secret. But Zeke can."

12

ZEKE

"What's taking them so long?" I ask, pacing to the front door again to peer out the peephole and hoping to see Siren and Lucy walking up the front steps. But just like the last dozen times, I don't see either of them.

"I'm sure they have a lot to talk about," Nora says.

I glare at her.

"You don't get to be pissy. You could have told Siren yourself the truth about Lucy. You chose not to. Now you have to deal with the consequences."

"Which are?"

"Only one of them is coming back alive," Nora says with a straight face.

I growl. "This is not the time for jokes."

She laughs. "They'll be fine."

I raise my eyebrows.

"Okay, so they probably won't be. But the worst that will happen is a catfight with nail scratches. They aren't going to really hurt each other."

I rub my neck. It's not just what they'll do to each other that worries me. I'm worried about Julian or Bishop coming after them. I'm worried about other untold danger, enemies hurting them. I shouldn't have let them go by themselves. I should have demanded I or one of the useless bodyguards go with them. Instead, they're drinking beer and watching a soccer game on their asses.

I feel Nora rubbing my back, her hands unable to reach my shoulders while I'm standing and her being so much smaller me.

"What are you doing?" I ask.

"Rubbing your back," Nora answers.

"Why?"

"Because you seem tense, and I'm trying to see what all the fuss is about. Lucy and Siren are right; you have great muscles, Zeke. What exercises do you do to get your back muscles to look like that?"

"I strangle people who annoy me with my bare hands," I answer.

Nora smiles but stops. "Fine, I was just trying to help. I'm going to order a pizza; I'm starving."

I stare at her wide-eyed. "I don't think it works that way here. We aren't in New York City or something. You can't just order a pizza to be delivered."

Nora sighs. "Fine, then I'm going to get food."

"No, you sure as hell aren't. It's not safe."

"Then, I'll bring one of the guys."

"You mean Beavis and Butthead? They are both drunk off their asses. They couldn't fight a fly right now and win," I say.

"Hey! Don't judge. You don't know us at all," Dylan says.

I run my hand through my hair, trying to keep calm. I really need to punch someone. Dylan will do. I don't understand why Siren hired them. It's like she was purposefully ensuring that Lucy wasn't safe, which pisses me off. Siren can hate Lucy, but she damn better respect that I care about Lucy and want her safe.

I throw a punch at Dylan without thinking.

"What the hell, man?" Jayden asks.

I throw a second with full intention of breaking his nose, but Dylan is prepared. He dodges me, the alcohol apparently not slowing him down.

"Easy man, we don't want to fight you," Dylan says.

"Well, too bad. If you'd done your damn job, then maybe I wouldn't have to fight you," I say back.

I take out Jayden's legs, and then finally land a punch to Dylan's face.

But I only angered a sleeping giant in both men. They fight back, hard. Harder than I expected for the two lazy drunks.

"Stop it before I hurt you," Dylan says.

I laugh. "You can't hurt me."

Just to prove a point, I let him punch me. I don't move. I'm a rock. A sheet of stone. A piece of solid steel.

Dylan blinks in surprise. "What's your problem?"

"My problem is you are supposed to be protecting Lucy, and instead, you are drunk watching a soccer game," I huff, shoving Dylan against the wall.

"Uh, Zeke. I don't know what they've been drinking, but it sure isn't alcohol. I've been drinking the same stuff, and I should be drunk right now, but instead, I'm sober," Nora says.

I stare at Jayden and then reach for the bottle to read it more carefully. It's non-alcoholic. I was wrong.

And then Dylan lands a punch that actually hurts. Not physically, but because I let my emotions cloud my judgments.

"And as for protecting Lucy, we've been watching her

on our phones. We have a man she doesn't know about who works at her favorite coffee shop. We spent the first week fighting her every time she went out to take us with, so we thought it'd be better to give her the illusion of independence when we are really watching her," Dylan says, thrusting his phone at me. "They are driving back, see?"

I do see. Both Lucy and Siren seem fine. Although, the redness and puffiness around both of their eyes scare me.

I fall back onto the couch. "I'm sorry."

Jayden shakes his head. "We understand, man. Lucy is special. And we've known Aria for a long time. She's one incredible woman."

I nod, trying to get my shit together and stop attacking everyone.

"I'm going to get you all some ice," Nora says.

"We're fine, ma'am. We are used to taking a hit," Dylan says.

Nora frowns. "I'm getting the ice. I don't want to look at a bruised nose and eye for however long we are here. And this way, I get to play nurse." She winks at Jayden before heading to the kitchen.

"Don't worry, boss. We won't let Nora affect our ability to do our jobs," Jayden says.

I nod, giving them the benefit of the doubt. Although, they don't know Nora like I do. If she wants to fuck them, she will, and she won't let them worrying about their job stand in her way.

"Give me your phone," I say to Dylan, needing to watch to ensure Siren and Lucy are okay the whole way here.

I sit on the couch and watch them drive in silence. I watch them park in front of the house. I resist the urge to run out the door and escort them inside.

"We brought dinner," Lucy says, as both women carry a bag into the room.

I stand up and take the bags from them, trying to read each of their faces, trying to see where they stand with me. But both of them hide their emotions well. I try to brush my fingers against Siren's, but she pulls away.

That's all I need to know. She's pissed.

Not that I blame her. I want time to talk alone, but there isn't anywhere in this house except the main bedroom to talk. And I feel weird taking Siren into the bedroom when it's Lucy's bedroom.

"Soup?" Nora asks.

"Borscht," Jayden responds. "Borscht is about the only thing we can get around here. It's why we are all so lean. It's the beet diet, guaranteed to make you lose weight."

Nora laughs. So does Lucy.

Siren is lost in thought.

"Hey, can we talk?" I ask Siren, needing a moment alone with her. Just a minute to connect. A second even. I'll take anything she gives me.

"We should eat. Don't want the soup getting even colder," Siren responds with a tight grin.

Nora meets my gaze and gives me an encouraging smile. Even Lucy notices Siren shutting me out, but Lucy gives me no clue as to how Siren feels about me.

We all get a bowl of soup, and then the three women sit on the couch, while the men eat the soup standing or on the floor as the TV gets changed to a rugby game.

"All we get are sports and news. What I wouldn't give to watch a good rom-com, a drama, a comedy—anything," Lucy says.

"You poor girl," Nora says, touching her arm. "I don't think I'd survive."

Lucy eyes Nora's Prada shoes, Balenciaga jeans, and Gucci shirt. "You wouldn't."

Both women laugh. Siren is lost in her bowl of soup. I want to go to her. Screw our audience. But Lucy catches my gaze and shakes her head, telling me to give her time.

So I do. It kills me, but I do.

The minutes tick by like hours. Hours like days. Finally, Lucy yawns, followed by Nora.

"Time for bed," Lucy announces.

Everyone mumbles their agreement.

Lucy stands and frowns. "Sorry, but I'm not giving up my bed. I have to live here a lot longer than one night, or however long you are planning on staying."

"Of course, you should get the bed," Nora says. "There doesn't happen to be a Park Hyatt or Four Seasons around here, does there?"

Lucy snorts.

The guys chuckle.

Nora sighs. "That's what I thought."

"There are two air mattresses the guys have been sleeping on and then, of course, the couch. There are blankets and pillows in the hall closet, but that's all I can offer you," Lucy says with a frown. She looks at me, asking if I want to share her bed like old times.

I glance over at Siren. It would make the sleeping arrangements easier for me and Lucy or me and Siren to share the queen in the only bedroom. But Lucy isn't offering her bed to me and Siren. I'll end up in bigger trouble if I sleep in the same bed as Lucy, even though nothing would happen.

I shake my head.

Lucy nods then disappears down the hallway.

"Aria and I can share the couch," Nora offers.

That leaves the two blowups.

"I'll sleep on the floor," I say.

Both men nod, and everyone gets to work making up the beds as best as they can with what we have. It feels like what I assume a frat house looks like after a night of partying. Everyone just finds what they can to use as a pillow, a blanket, a bed. And then a few moments later, everyone is asleep. Well, almost everyone.

I'm awake.

And so is Siren.

"Siren?" I say from my spot on the floor, hoping she's awake. I'm hoping for more than that; I'm hoping she's willing to talk to me.

"I'm awake, Zeke," she answers after two beats.

She spoke.

"Can we talk?" I ask, my voice hesitant.

"Isn't that what we are doing now? Talking?"

I sigh. She's not going to make this easy.

"Did Lucy tell you the truth?" I ask.

A breath.

"Yes."

There is a lot of emotion in that yes. A lot of pain. A lot of fear. And, if I look closely, love. At least I hope there is still love.

"Good, you needed to hear Lucy's truth."

"What about yours?" Siren asks.

"I'll tell you anything you want to know."

"Did you love her when you were teenagers? When you were fucking? Were you in love with her?"

"Yes, I loved her." I swallow, hoping my words don't cause Siren any more suffering.

"Were you devastated when you lost..." she clears her throat. "When you lost the baby?"

I close my eyes, feeling that pain for the first time in years. *It hurt, but was I devastated?*

"No. It hurt, but I felt relief. I wasn't ready to be a father." I wait for what I assume is going to be her next question. *Am I ready to be a father now?* I don't know how to answer that.

"Are you still in love with her?" Siren asks the most important question instead.

I smile. This question, I know how to answer. But I'm not answering it from the floor where she can't see the truth in my eyes.

I stand up, looming over Siren, who has been staring up at a water damaged ceiling. She's picking at a thread on the blanket nervously.

She stops when she sees me.

"No, I'm not still in love with Lucy. I love her like a friend, a sister. I would protect her with my life. But I'm not in love with her."

Siren lets out a whoosh of a breath.

"I can't love her because my heart is already taken. I'm in love with you, Siren. I wasn't lying when I called you my forever. Even if we separated, even if you stopped loving me, my heart wouldn't stop. I'd love you forever. You're it for me."

A tear rolls down her cheek. Then I lift her off the couch, catching the tear with my lips as I cradle her in my arms.

"You're it for me, forever," I whisper into her hair, feeling whole again with her in my arms.

"You're my forever too. My anchor. My love."

We kiss. The kind of kiss needed to heal old wounds. But somehow the kiss opens more wounds than it closes. It opens the pain of letting Lucy slip from my life, at losing a baby, a future. The pain at knowing Lucy was in danger.

The kiss pulls me and Siren closer together while also pushing us apart. We are both desperate to be together. To stay together. To love each other forever. But the harder we fight for that, the more it feels like we are also slipping from each other. This thing between us can't last. Any time either of us has loved before, it didn't last. It ended.

I carry Siren to the hallway; it's as much privacy as we are going to get.

"Will you tell me about the secret? What are you protecting for Lucy?" Siren asks.

"Yes, I just can't here."

She nods. "I don't want you to here. I just want to know that you will. Right now, all I want is you."

13

SIREN

Zeke still loves me. I could cry. Jump for joy. Do all the things that most people take for granted. He loves me, that's all that matters.

His past with Lucy doesn't matter any more than my past with Hugo matters. At one point, I loved Hugo. And at one point, Zeke loved Lucy.

But this thing between us is different. This thing kept us both awake all night. This thing has ended in us making out in a dark hallway like two horny teenagers trying not to wake their parents up. Except instead of parents, we are trying not to wake up Zeke's ex-lover, my best friend, and two bodyguards.

None of them even enter my mind when Zeke starts kissing down my neck with just the right about of pressure and just enough tongue to make my insides tingle.

"Zeke, we can't," I say, trying to hold onto my fleeting logic.

"We can't what?" Zeke says. "Do this?" He grabs my bottom lip with teeth as he pushes my shirt up my stomach until he finds my bare breasts. I'm not wearing a bra, which right now, I'm thankful for. It gives Zeke good access without having to get completely naked in case someone gets up in the middle of the night to pee or something.

Bathroom! We should move to the bathroom.

But then Zeke's head drops, and he's sucking, licking, tormenting my nipple, and I forget about my idea.

My shirt is up around my neck. So much for decency if someone comes into the hallway.

"Bathroom," I mumble, my head dazed, my eyes barely able to focus. Instead, they keep rolling back in my head as Zeke slides his tongue down my chest and over my stomach, dipping down into my pants before he stops.

His hand finds its way between the waistband of my pajamas and underwear, cupping my pussy, just resting his hand, letting me know what he could do, but not giving it to me yet.

He gives me a wicked grin. "I'm tired of bathrooms. Too small."

And then one finger slides inside me. I groan, my back arches against the wall as my nails dig into the nape of Zeke's neck.

"Don't scream, Siren. Not unless you want to wake everyone up and let them find you naked."

"I'm not naked—"

But then, I am. My shirt is gone; my pants and underwear hang around my ankles. I'm naked in the hallway, feet away from where four other people are sleeping.

Zeke raises an eyebrow as if to dare me to tell him to stop. Tell him this isn't happening. Tell him that I don't want this.

I can't. I want this. After my conversation with Lucy, after every painful thing she said, I can't not have Zeke. I need the connection. I need to know he still chooses me, no matter what else is going on.

"You have no idea how worried I was when you were gone," Zeke says, as if reading my thoughts.

He grabs my cheeks, holding my head as he stares down at me and kisses me tenderly on the lips.

"Yea? Worried I was going to hurt Lucy?"

He frowns, his eyes darkening into slits. "No, I was worried you would get hurt."

We kiss. Our lips and tongues meld together as his erection, still locked away in his pants, pushes at my stomach.

"I'm a tough girl, I don't get hurt easily," I say, lifting the hem up his shirt up and tossing it to the ground so I can I feel every rippling muscle of his against my skin.

"I know you can take care of yourself, but there are dangerous men out there," he says, taking my nipple in his mouth again.

I curse, probably too loudly, but it feels too good not to express exactly how I feel.

"Dangerous men are my specialty," I say.

Zeke bites down.

I yelp.

"I'm not just worried about you getting hurt by dangerous men. I didn't want Lucy to... I mean, I didn't want..."

He stops licking my nipples and looks me dead in the eyes. He was scared he was going to lose me. But that was the risk he was willing to take. He needed me to know the truth. He needed me to know how serious he is about us.

"Make love to me against the wall Zeke. Love me hard and fast like you're the only man in the world who could ever satisfy me. It's the truth. I want you; no other man will do. Just you."

He smiles. "Just you, forever."

And then we aren't calm anymore. I'm ripping off his pants as he lifts one of my legs up and thrusts into my aching pussy. I arch my back, accepting all of him, needing this more than I need air after my conversation with Lucy.

There are more conversations to have. More truths. More sins. But I have no doubt that through it all, there will be love.

This cements it. Here in this dirty, filthy hallway. In the darkness. Us both naked connecting in a way we've done dozens of times before. But lately, each time we fuck, it becomes more and more magical. More and more important.

This time is no different. I can see it in Zeke's eyes. I can feel it in the way he glides in and out of me. The intensity of our kisses. The carnalness of our groans. It's everywhere. It's inescapable.

And it's scary as fuck.

I won't be able to escape Zeke. Even if he hurts me, even if he stops loving me, he'll still be there. He'll keep haunting me. Living with me. The love we are forming won't just leave because I need it to. It won't vanish because we are over each other.

It will remain forever.

Somehow, each time we say the word, each time we promise forever, it gets a little less scary. A little less daunting. Forever is only scary when you haven't found the right person. With Zeke Kane, I've found more than the right person. I've found everything.

"Zeke," I dig my nails into his back, trying to hold onto him as much as I'm holding onto this moment. These few minutes where I feel right. Where I feel like we finally found the right person in the right moment at the right time. This moment feels like destiny.

"Forever," he whispers against my hair softly, before biting down hard drawing blood.

Forever.

We both come hard and fast, holding onto each other terrified that after this moment ends, everything will change. That the promises we made to each other will mean nothing. And that's a scary thought. If we can't keep this promise to each other, we are doomed.

We both take a deep breath and exhale, calmer now than if we had just spent the entire day meditating.

"Gross."

"Disgusting."

Zeke and I both freeze, staring at each other like we just got caught by our parents. Really we just got caught by Nora and Lucy.

"Get a room," Nora says, walking toward the bathroom. "Although, that ass...momma like."

I snarl. "Go to the bathroom and leave us alone."

Nora wiggles her eyebrows while staring at Zeke's bare ass. Zeke just laughs, watching my reaction to Nora.

"It is a good ass," he says with a wink.

My face reddens.

I see Lucy out of the corner of my eye, smirking at the two of us. "You do realize I heard you the entire time, right?"

I wince. "Thanks for letting us finish first," I say, my voice ringing higher and chipper than it should.

Lucy shakes her head, but she's smiling. "You owe me," she says.

I nod. *I do.*

But then she tilts her head, taking in Zeke's ass.

My pleasant mood disappears.

"It is a really a good ass," she sighs, turning away. "If you stay tomorrow night, you can have my room. But you are washing the sheets and getting me a new mattress afterward."

Lucy disappears into her bedroom. Nora takes her sweet time in the bathroom.

I look up into Zeke's eyes, and I no longer care. His eyes don't see Nora or Lucy. They don't even acknowledge we were just interrupted. His eyes only see me.

He tucks a strand of hair behind my ear and kisses my forehead. All of my anxiety vanishes.

"Are you jealous that they saw my ass?" he asks.

"They saw more than just your ass," I say.

"Yea, they saw how much I'm in love with you."

"Definitely."

14

ZEKE

SIREN FALLS asleep in my arms as I lean against the base of the couch. Nora is fast asleep on the couch. Dylan and Jayden are fast asleep on the blow-ups. All three of them are snoring. I should be in hell, leaning against a broken couch on a cold floor, unable to sleep.

But I'm in heaven. Siren is snuggled against me, and she's mine. She's really mine. I feel it. I know it. This time, I won't lose her. This time, instead of fighting, we will work together. This time we will be able to get free of the monsters of our past.

And then what?

I don't have a clue. *Go back to working for Enzo Black, probably?* Even that isn't required for me to be happy.

This is all I require. Siren in my arms. Siren relying on me. Siren letting me protect her, love her.

Siren starts snoring as well. I bite back a laugh at how adorable she is.

I won't be able to sleep in this position. I can't stretch my legs fully out without hitting the wall. My head is too high and can't rest on the back of the couch. I don't care, though. I plan on watching Siren sleep all night. Or maybe I'll wake her up in an hour or two, and we can fuck in the hallway or bathroom again, before everyone wakes up. Yea, that sounds like a good plan. Nora and Lucy scolded us for doing it earlier, so there's nothing they haven't seen or heard from us. *What does it matter if we get caught again?*

But right now, Siren is peaceful. I wouldn't dare wake her up, not when she seems so content, so happy. Something so rare for her—to have a moment where she isn't worrying or having to protect others. She's just herself.

Tomorrow, we have a lot to figure out. I've shared Lucy with Siren. Siren knows everything. Well, almost everything. She knows the painful parts. The rest is more about me trusting her to continue to keep Lucy safe. I already trust her, even though Siren and Lucy will never be best friends. *How could they?* They were both in love with me at different points. It's natural for them to fight over me a little, even though Lucy and I have long since gone our separate ways.

We can't keep staying here. Siren and I being around Lucy is only putting her at risk. She can't stay here, though. She needs to move somewhere safe, and someplace she can tolerate better than this freezing country.

Once we move Lucy somewhere safe, the hard part begins. Figuring out a way to destroy Julian, Bishop, and any other men the two are connected to.

I hug Siren closer to my chest. Her lips part, and a tiny drop of drool drops on my chest.

God, I could get used to this.

I stroke her hair and kiss her forehead. I'll protect you. I promise I'll protect you no matter what.

We can destroy Julian, Bishop, and every other enemy we have, together. But we are only strong together.

I let my eyes fall closed for a moment. Of course, the only together moments I'm thinking about are Siren naked, her nipples puckered, her hips rolling meeting mine as my cock drives into her.

What I wouldn't give for a bed. *When's the last time Siren and I fucked in a bed? Not a bathroom, hallway, or alleyway?*

I want to go back to St. Kitts, back to Julian's property, just so we have a bed I can claim her in again. A bed that's mine. *No, a bed that's ours.*

I won't be able to sleep in a bed again without Siren by my side. Hopefully, naked and ready to ride my cock. And in the morning, getting woken up with her smart mouth, knowing if I fuck up, if I hurt her in any way, she'd have no problem using a knife or gun to set me straight again.

Siren is what I've been searching for all this time. An equal. A woman I can love and protect, but who doesn't need my protection. If I was with a woman who couldn't protect herself, I would spend my entire life worrying. I'd never be able to leave her alone.

I still worry about Siren but in a healthy sense. I worry about her because I love her. I'm not crippled with worry, though.

I can close my eyes and know she's safe. I can let her go and know she will come back to me. I can even let her face her own enemies alone, knowing if something happens, she can protect herself until I can get to her—not that I will ever allow that to happen again.

My eyes fly open from my unsettling thoughts. But I'm not the only one who is unsettled.

Siren is twitching in my arms. She's been deep in sleep for over an hour, but now she's restless. She moans and starts thrashing. She's having a nightmare.

"Siren, baby, I got you. You're safe," I whisper into her ear.

She doesn't stop.

Dammit.

"Siren," I say louder, holding her against my chest tightly, hoping my comfort will be enough to settle her back into a restful sleep.

"No," she groans, still asleep.

"Siren!" I yell, not caring about waking up the entire house. I can't keep watching her struggle in her nightmare.

But it's not enough. I shake her. I say her name over and over. I tap her cheek. I consider getting up and splashing water on her face, surely that would do the trick. But just before I'm about to get up to get the water, Siren's eyes fly open.

It takes her a minute to adjust to reality and get out of her dream. When she finally does, she says, "He's here."

I shake my head, not understanding. "You're safe. I'm here. Zeke's here."

Siren blinks up at me rapidly, but my presence doesn't seem to make her feel safer. In fact, she seems more concerned that I'm here. I'm not sure if it's because she thinks I'm the enemy, or if she doesn't want me to be in harm's way.

I don't have time to ask her. I don't get to ask what her nightmare was about, or what premonition she had about who is here. Suddenly, the familiar sound of gunfire thrusts me into action.

I push Siren down instinctively, protecting her with my body.

Dylan and Jayden jump up, their internal alarms going off as well at the sound we've all faced numerous times.

They have guns in their hands and are firing back through the windows.

"We'll get Lucy," Dylan says, and they're both running toward Lucy.

Lucy will be safe, I repeat to myself. They are both good men, good guards. I just hope they are great shots as well.

Nora stirs on the couch.

"Get down!" I shout at her.

She ducks, just as a bullet flies over her head, barely missing her.

Fuck, that was close.

I reach for my gun and start shooting back through the windows, but I can't see who is shooting at us, not without getting closer to the windows, closer to the danger.

The first task is to get everyone to safety, the second task is to get rid of the threat, and the final task is finding out who is attacking us.

"Go to the bedroom, both of you," I shout to Nora and Siren. "I've got this."

Nora scrambles off the couch.

"And keep your head down, crawl if you have to," I shout, firing again, hoping it provides enough protection for Nora to make it to the bedroom. There is only one small window in that room. It will be safer than the front of the house.

There has to be more than a dozen men firing at us, something I've dealt with hundreds of times. I can take them down, but it will take some time. In the meantime, Lucy, Nora, and Siren aren't safe in this house.

I feel Siren moving behind me. *Please, obey my orders for once.*

She moves out from behind me. "I'll cover you, go back and protect Nora," I say, hoping that reminding her to protect her friend will be enough to get her out of harm's way.

"I'm not falling for that," Siren says, her gun out and firing through the window on the other side of the house. She's wearing pajama pants and a tank top. No bra. Her hair is disheveled. She's barefoot. She couldn't be less protected, but she looks fierce as fuck.

I can't argue with her about wearing more protective clothing. I'm wearing my boxers, and that's it.

"This will be over much faster if we both fight. I'll take the left side of the house, you take the right," she orders.

Dammit, I curse under my breath as she runs off toward the left side of the house. She crouches low as she moves, her gun raised and firing when she gets a chance. A bullet flies in, and she moves easily out of the way before it has a chance to hit her.

Siren is strong. That's one of the many reasons I love her. She can protect herself. *Go do what you do best, destroy these motherfuckers.*

I glide effortlessly through the string of bullets to the right window. My eyes cut through the broken glass, peering out at my enemies. There are two men by a tree.

I wait for the bullets to spray in, and then I fire back, hitting the two men square in the chest. *Pop. Pop.*

I wait. More bullets are fired, but I can't see where they're coming from.

I roll under the window to get a better angle. Spotting two more men, both are dead with two more shots.

Most people don't understand why I do what I do. *Yes, I love protecting people.* I feel good knowing that I protect my friends, my family. But that isn't the only reason I do this. It's been a long time since I've been in a gunfight.

There is nothing like the high. Nothing like the adrenaline pulsing through my body as I take on my enemy, not knowing if I'm going to live or die. Although, I already know the outcome, and that's my secret. I may not act like a cocky asshole in every area of my life, but when it comes to doing my job, I'm as cocky as it gets. I know I'm going to kill them all. Mercilessly, and without a second thought.

I'm going to win. I'm going to walk out of here without a scratch. It's the only way to do this job. If you don't already know you are going to win, then you won't be able to step out into battle. You won't be able to risk everything.

The bullets slow. Only one left on my side. I don't know how Siren is doing. We shouldn't kill them all. If we do, we have no one to torture. No one to tell us who they are working for and why they are here. We can find out other ways, but there is nothing easier than torturing someone. Very few people can handle the pain. All it takes is a broken finger, a knife to the stomach, a twist of the neck to make people talk.

I take a deep breath. Keeping people alive can be the hardest part of the job. Disabling them, but keeping them alive so I can torture them. I have to hit them in just the right spot. Avoid major arteries or organs so they don't bleed out and die before I get to them. I don't want them to think they are actually dying. A dying man can be at peace more than a living man. A dying man stops feeling pain. A dying man lets go; he doesn't surrender.

Unless he's a pussy. Unless he's scared of death. Very few men in this world are, though.

I see the last man behind a car. It's not an easy shot from this angle. His head is in clear view, but a head shot almost always ends in death or paralysis. I need him alive.

I aim for his shoulder, knowing one slip and I'd hit his heart. Game over.

I take a deep breath, readying myself for the shot, keeping my body calm and relaxed.

And then...*pop*.

I look to my left. I didn't fire the shot, Siren did.

I blink rapidly.

"You would have hit his heart. You were too tight, not relaxed. We needed him alive," she says.

I look at the man, who has fallen to the ground gripping his bleeding hand. The gun has fallen out of it. She hit him right in the hand.

"Come on," she says, jumping out the window, breaking the remaining glass as she does. I follow after her, watching as she calmly walks toward the man. He reaches for his gun, but she fires at his other hand, stopping him from ever being able to hold anything again.

Siren is fucking incredible as she walks with all the confidence in the world. That cockiness you need in a gunfight, that knowledge to trust your instincts—Siren has that in spades.

I speed my steps up, so I reach the man at the same time she does.

"Who do you work for?" I ask in my husky, take no prisoners, no bullshit voice. Siren could have asked him, but my voice is deeper, more powerful sounding than hers.

She folds her arms, not the least bit upset that I spoke first. She knows I'm more likely to get him to talk than she is.

The man starts crying, holding both of his hands against his chest.

Fuck, I hate the cryers.

Siren rolls her eyes and looks at me. We both know that if we were in his position, we'd die with dignity. We wouldn't mention our boss's name, and we wouldn't be crying like a coward.

I raise an eyebrow at Siren, excited to play bad cop, good cop with her. *I'll hurt him; you comfort him.* Siren just huffs and kneels in front of him, gripping his neck tightly in her hand.

I smirk. *Yea, like Siren could ever be the good cop.* She's just a fierce as I am. Somehow when she speaks, her voice comes out like honey. "Tell us who your boss is, and I'll kill you instead of Zeke. Trust me, you want me to be the one who kills you. I'm the better shot. I'll kill you cleanly. Zeke over here, he's pissed. You ruined a perfect night for him. The kind where you have perfect sex and have a half-naked woman drapes over you all night, with the promise of a good morning fuck. You feel me? You ruined that for my man here. He's not going to let you die an easy, quick death. So, again, who do you work for?"

He shudders and weeps at Siren's words. She releases him, obviously disgusted by his weakness. She looks at me, allowing me a turn.

I don't want to torture men in front of Siren. I don't want her to be afraid of me, but I don't really have a choice. We need answers. We need to know who is coming after us.

I shoot Siren a warning look to look away if she's at all squeamish about blood and pain. She's seen her fair share, but this is different. This is me torturing a helpless man to get information. She's seen me hurt Hugo, but we want answers fast. There are two ways to do that. Both end in a lot of blood and screams.

She nods.

And then I do it. I pull a knife from my pocket. "Last chance," I threaten low and commanding, my voice so calm, it scares most men when I get in this mode.

"I can't," his voice trembles. He can't because his boss would kill him. Whoever his boss is, he isn't as bad as I am.

Not when someone threatens people that I love. This man just threatened two women I love, Siren's best friend, and two loyal guards. This man is about to see how vile I can truly get.

I hold the knife to his eye, summoning everything into my action: my anger, my fear, my love. I jab the knife into his eye. His screams are high and retched. The kind that tell me this is as bad as it gets. No physical pain can be worse. Although, I can think of a lot of worse things. A whole fucking lot.

I look over at Siren, who is watching me carefully. Worse than a knife to the eye is losing a woman you love because you had to torture a man viciously to keep her safe.

Finally, I pull the eyeball free from his socket. Blood goes everywhere, along with puss, and god knows what oozing from the socket. Most people would vomit at the sight, but it's one of my favorite tricks. It's easy to do and is almost a hundred percent effective. And I prefer it to the other option that is usually a hundred percent effective —castration.

"Who do you work for?" I ask, dancing the knife across his cheek toward the other eye, threatening completely remove his sight.

The man is sobbing now. He cringes away at the knife on his face. He's pissed his pants.

Oh, Jesus. Maybe I should have gone with something easier. I may have just scared him into not being able to talk. The tongue can also be an effective torture device.

"Bi—," the man finally cries out but then collapses.

Siren and I exchange glances, not entirely sure what he was about to say, but guessing he meant Bishop.

Siren leans down to check his pulse. "He's gone."

"Do you think he meant Bishop?"

She nods.

Fuck.

I take a deep breath and look at Siren, afraid she's never going to be able to get over what I just did to that man.

She laughs at my expression.

"What?" I ask.

"You're scared," she says matter of factly.

I nod.

"You think me watching you cut out a man's eye makes me think less of you? Makes me think of you as an evil man?"

I nod again. *That about covers it.*

She shakes her head with a smile. "I usually find seduction works well to get a man to talk when I have the time. I get more information that way."

"I'll keep that in mind, although, most men don't find me very attractive."

She laughs and then throws her arms around my neck. She raises up on her tiptoes, so our lips are almost pressed together. "And I can't be mad at you for something I've done before. Although, your technique might be better. You've probably had more practice. I usually just go for the balls."

"Is it wrong to say that's so fucking hot?"

She shakes her head and brushes her lips over mine. "No, it just means we are perfect for each other."

We kiss, the kind of hungry, desperate kiss, reassuring each other that we are okay. We are unhurt. Somehow, we are even more in love.

"Zeke," I hear Lucy's desperate voice from behind me, instantly chilling any heat between Siren and me.

"I think Dylan...I think he's dead," Lucy says.

Dammit. I didn't know the man for more than twenty-four hours, but he seemed like a good man. He didn't deserve to die like this.

Siren grabs my hand, and we race inside, both hoping Lucy's wrong. Hoping he isn't dead, and we weren't making out while a good man was dying.

15

SIREN

"Fuck!" Zeke yells as he does chest compressions on Dylan.

I count with him and then give Dylan breaths in between Zeke's compressions. We both know Dylan is dead, but we've seen people come back from the dead before, so we don't stop. Not when we both feel guilty. He's dead because of us. We weren't fast enough.

It's one of the many reasons why Zeke and I have never fallen in love before. It puts our job at risk. We can't do as good of a job when we are thinking of each other, instead of the people we should be protecting.

So we keep trying. Zeke hammers into Dylan's chest. I try everything to breathe life into his lungs. And we both ignore Nora and Lucy's sobs as they hold each other in the corner.

"He's dead," Jayden says, standing over us, trying to get us to stop.

Jayden puts a hand on my shoulder, knowing Zeke is too focused. Zeke doesn't lose men. I'm the one who is going to need to convince Zeke to stop.

I sit back on my heels with tears in my eyes. Dylan was a

good man, a good worker. He was always someone I could call when I needed someone for a job. It kills me to feel responsible for his death.

"Shit," I curse, wiping my mouth and gripping my hair at the scalp.

"It's time. We have to go, or we will have more death on our hands," Jayden says, looking at a terrified Nora and Lucy.

I nod. *I can do this.*

"Zeke, we have to go," I say, gently touching his shoulder.

"Not yet, I can bring him back," Zeke says, pumping over him.

"Zeke, we have others to protect," I say.

Zeke frowns. "I can't. I don't let men die. I don't—"

"Zeke," I demand. "We have to go, now." My voice is firm and loud.

Zeke looks up at me, his face full of pain matching my own. But I don't let my pain out. Zeke can't see my pain. He needs to see the machine. He needs to see that we have to keep going. We have more people to protect. We failed, but we can't fail again.

I hold out my hand. Zeke takes it reluctantly.

I look to Jayden. "Car?"

He nods. "Follow me."

Jayden leads us into the bedroom, pushes the bed out of the way, and lifts a hatch to an underground tunnel.

Zeke and I eliminated the immediate threat. But if Bishop is smart, he'll have more men coming. Or he'll be tracking us. So it's safer to disappear down a tunnel then head back out to the main street.

Jayden hops down.

"Go," I say to Lucy and Nora.

Both eye the gun I've picked up carefully. "I won't let anything happen to either of you," I promise them.

They nod, and then follow Jayden down. I pick up Zeke's gun and hand it to him.

"Let's make good on my promise," I tell him.

He nods, back in protection mode. We both follow, ready to shoot anyone who follows us, but no one does.

We clomp through a dirty tunnel, exit through a hidden door at the end, and hop into the parked van just outside.

"Where to?" Jayden asks.

"The small private airfield. I'll arrange a plane, but..." Zeke starts.

He can't pay for it.

"But I don't have the money. I'm going to have to borrow more from you, Nora," Zeke finally says. He spent all of his money saving me.

"Take my money," Lucy says.

"Luce, I couldn't," Zeke says.

"You're using it to save my life. Take my money—all of it. As much as you need," Lucy says.

I bite my lip to keep from saying something bitchy. "Lucy, I don't want to sound like a bitch, but a private plane and fuel could cost hundreds of thousands of dollars on such short notice."

Lucy smirks. "I'm worth a hundred million. I think I can afford it."

My mouth drops. *What?*

Nora's eyes go wide, the shock of seeing a man die fading as Lucy admits her net worth.

"How?" Nora asks.

I glance at Zeke, but he doesn't seem surprised in the least. He reaches behind him to where Lucy is sitting next to Nora in the van.

"Thank you," he squeezes her hand. "I'll pay you back."

She shakes her head, squeezing his hand back. "No, pay me back by protecting us."

"I promise," he says. Then Zeke is on the phone making last-minute arrangements to get us an airplane. Lucy starts barking bank account numbers at him.

I notice Nora in the corner, shaking. "I can't fly."

I frown, seeing how nervous she is. "Yes, you can."

She shakes. "I can't. I'm having a panic attack."

I grab her hand. "Then we will do it together." I don't have a clue how to fly a plane, but I have no doubt Nora can do this. She just needs a little encouragement. She's a kick-ass, strong woman.

Zeke stares down at me, with worry in his eyes as he finishes the call. "You're bleeding."

I look down to my ribcage, where blood is trickling out of my tank top. Then I see Zeke's arm.

"So are you."

He frowns. We don't have time to deal with our wounds now; neither one is life-threatening. I tell him with my eyes we are both fine, we just need to get on the plane and then we can take care of each other's wounds.

He nods reluctantly. He stares down, and for a second, I think he's going to take his boxers off to try and tie around my wound to put pressure on it.

I laugh and shake my head. That's not going to happen, but it warms my heart what he's willing to do to make sure I'm okay. That I'm safe.

Jayden drives us to the tarmac where a plane sits.

"I can't fly that," Nora says as we pull up.

I turn around and take her hand again. "Yes, you can. I'll be there with you the whole way to keep you calm. You've flown hundreds of times; you got this. Just take your time.

We already took out the bad guys. Any others coming won't be here for a while." I tell her the truth, mostly. At least I don't think we are being followed or will need to make a quick getaway. For now, my job is to keep Nora calm and collected. Get her on the plane, into the cockpit, and then her instincts will take over.

Nora shakes her head. "No. I mean, I can't fly that plane as in I don't know how. That's a different type of plane requiring a different type of license. It's bigger than any plane I usually fly. It's different. I don't have the training to fly this plane."

I spot Zeke stiffen out of the corner of my eye. We may not be followed right now, but we shouldn't fly commercial. We will be tracked. And Zeke wasn't able to hire a pilot on such short notice.

We could try to find a different pilot, my raised eyebrows tell him.

His eyes scream the urgency of our situation.

I nod. *We need to leave now.*

"What do you need to be able to fly this plane?" I ask, staring at Nora.

"Um...I'm not sure."

"Let's get you into the cockpit and see what you think," I say.

Nora exhales a sharp breath. "This definitely isn't legal."

I smirk. Nora never breaks the rules. She never has to. Her money, good looks, and status always allow her to get away with anything.

Zeke throws the door open to frigid air, still only in his boxers.

"I'll call to see how long it would take to get a pilot here, but if she can fly this thing, it would be better," Zeke says.

I agree. It would involve fewer questions and be less likely we would be followed.

I grab Nora's hand and pull her out of the van with me.

Jayden and Lucy follow, with Jayden holding Lucy tightly and scanning for any attackers. I'm beginning to think she has a bigger part in all of this than I understand. If she is worth as much money as she says she is, it had to come from somewhere. Even if she was an executive at some coffee company, she wouldn't be worth a hundred million.

But I don't have time to ask more questions about Lucy or ask Zeke what the secret was that he never had time to tell me. We have a plane to fly.

I drag Nora into the cockpit, knowing Zeke and Jayden will handle everything else.

My eyes fly wide, and my mouth falls open as I stare at the panel in front of me.

"Holy shit," I say, blinking rapidly and hoping I'm not seeing what I'm seeing. I understand now why Nora said she couldn't fly it. I've sat in cockpits numerous times in Nora's plane. It's like the difference between driving a cardboard car and a Ferrari. It's not even comparable.

There are hundreds of buttons and switches on this jet, compared to the dozen on her propeller plane.

Nora hops into the seat, trying to appear confident.

"I need you to sit in that seat and do exactly as I tell you," Nora says.

I nod, sitting down calmly. *Maybe she has this.*

Nora stares wide-eyed at the buttons, not touching any of them.

"If you can't, it's okay. We will find someone else," I say. I'd rather take my chances in a gunfight than be thousands of feet in the air and not be able to land.

"Um..." Zeke says suddenly from behind us. "How is it going?"

"Not that well," I say.

He looks at me with concern. "Then, I'm going to need you to bandage that up and grab your gun."

"Why?"

"Because Jayden spotted a car coming at us quick, less than a mile out," Zeke answers.

They are here—Bishop's men.

I pat Nora on the shoulder. "Get in the back and hide. We will take out these men and find another pilot or way out of here."

"No, I'm not hiding. Not again. I'll be here, figuring out how to fly this thing," Nora says.

I want to argue with her, but instead, I nod, gritting my teeth. I want to demand she move to the back of the plane where it's safer, but I don't know if we are going to be able to take out the men this time. Who knows how many are coming.

If Nora can get us off the ground, we will worry about landing later.

16

ZEKE

"Siren!" I holler into the cockpit as I load our guns with ammunition, staring out the door at the car barreling toward us, filled with angry men seeking revenge for their fallen co-workers. They will face the same fate, though.

"You want a shirt to put on?" Jayden asks me, loading his own weapons calmly like the professional he is, not like a man who just lost his friend and is about to go into battle again.

"Why? You going to let me borrow yours?" I ask.

Jayden smiles. "Not a chance in hell. You'd stretch it out."

I grin. "I would. I don't think we have any shirts handy anyway."

"Don't put on a shirt or pants. I think the wild Tarzan look works for you. You're much scarier without a shirt," Siren says with a wink.

We are all being playful, trying to keep things light, even though we know the seriousness we are about to face.

I stare at the blood covering Siren's shirt. "Any luck with finding a first aid kit?" I ask Lucy in the back of the plane.

She frowns. "Not yet."

I sigh and walk over to Siren. I kneel in front of her, and she grins like I'm about to propose instead of ruin her clothes. I grab her pant leg and rip it in half around the knee. And then I stand and wrap the fabric around her chest, tying it off, so it covers the wound in her side and hopefully reduces the bleeding.

It won't help if her adrenaline starts pumping fast, and we have to move or run, but it's better than nothing.

"Thanks," Siren says with heat in her eyes.

"That wasn't meant to be sexy," I whisper against her lips, my hand dipping behind her head, holding it in place as my thumb brushes over her bottom lip.

"Taking care of me is incredibly sexy," she says back, licking her lip.

I bite my lip as I feel my cock get hard. "There is nothing more enjoyable than going into a fight with a hard-on. Thank you for that."

"At least it will be entertaining," she says.

"Guys," Jayden says.

We both drop our smiles and pick up our guns. We're all crouched inside the plane, peering out the single door as the van drives onto the tarmac, followed by three more cars.

We have the high point and will be able to shoot down at them, but we are sitting ducks. We can't move unless Nora figures out how to get us off the ground. And if they have a bomb, we're screwed.

"Ready for round two?" I ask.

"Yes," Siren and Jayden say at the same time.

"Good, let's finish this," I say, even though I suspect whoever these people are, it's only the beginning.

The car parks, and we all aim. But only a single man steps out, his arms raised in surrender.

"Hold fire," I say to Siren and Jayden.

They continue to aim their guns at the man, but neither of them shoot.

"Give us Lucy, and we will go," the man says.

"No way in hell," I yell back.

The man shakes his head. "This isn't your fight. Give us Lucy. We won't harm her. You know that. Give us Lucy, and you are free to go."

Shit.

I spot Lucy in the back of the plane, inching forward, like she's willing to turn herself over to save us.

"I made a promise, and I plan on keeping that promise," I scold Lucy.

I ignore Siren's stare and need to understand the final piece of Lucy's and my relationship. I turn my attention back to the negotiator.

"No. But I'm giving you one chance to surrender—one chance to turn around and leave. If you stay and fight, you are all dead. Just ask your friends scattered about in our front lawn."

He sneers. "I'll ask your dead friend."

I shoot. So do Siren and Jayden. I'm not one to start a fight. I usually wait for the enemy to attack first. When I kill them, I can tell myself it was all in self-defense. But this time, it's not just about protection. It's about revenge.

We fire, taking down man after man as soon as they step out of the car. We are going to win easily.

But then I see more cars coming—dozens. I see one with a man standing out the sunroof with a rocket launcher on his shoulder.

"Shit. Nora, how is it coming up there?" I ask, listening to the engines purr to life. At least she got them started.

"It's coming!" Nora says.

I turn to Siren, and we exchange worried expressions. In this field, you always have a plan A through Z. You almost never get to stick to plan A. We need more plans. If they fire a rocket at us, we are all screwed.

"They won't," Siren says.

I frown. "Why not?"

"They want Lucy. We would all be dead if they fired that at us," she answers.

She's right.

They want Lucy. *But would they rather have her dead than us escape with her?* Once again, I glance at Lucy. I reassure her with my eyes that I'm going to protect her, no matter what.

"Fuck," Siren curses as a bullet grazes her cheek. She rolls back, hiding behind the metal frame of the plane.

"Siren?"

"I'm fine," she says.

Fine—fuck, I hate that word. And I hate that I was paying attention to Lucy instead of protecting Siren.

It's then that I realize I'm not going to be able to save everyone, definitely not everyone I made promises to.

I fire more shots, trying to focus on winning the battle.

"What's plan B?" Jayden asks, firing next to me.

I have a plan B, but Siren isn't going to like it.

"No," Siren says beside me, reading my mind. I could charge forward as a diversion while they all slipped out the back and hopefully steal one of the nearby cars.

"What's plan C?" Jayden asks as we continue to fire, but for every man we take down, more show up.

"I become the diversion instead," Siren says.

"Nope," I say, not even considering it.

"Well, I guess I might as well offer myself up as a diversion then," Jayden says.

"No, we aren't going to sacrifice anyone in order for the others to escape," I say.

"Plan E, then?" Jayden asks.

"Plan E is we fly the hell out of here," Nora shouts, and the plane lurches forward.

"Holy shit," Siren curses, looking me in the eye. She's not sure if she's happy or scared to death we are moving. If we are moving, it means Nora is going to attempt to fly this thing. That only ends two ways—us flying away safely, or us crashing to our deaths. There is no middle ground.

I grab her hand, and we lock fingers as we continue to shoot as the plane moves to the runway. One of the cars follows, but it's a futile attempt.

"Lock that door and put your seatbelts on," Nora yells, her voice full of determination.

"Can she really fly this thing? It's huge!" Jayden asks.

"Do you have a plan F?" I ask.

He stares out the window at all the cars of men waiting for us to turn around or crash so they can kill us.

"Nope," he answers.

"Then we are going with plan E," I say.

"God, help us all," Jayden says, making his way to the back where Lucy is. I hear him mumble to her about the back is actually the safest spot on an airplane and how to brace if we crash.

I look at Siren, still gripping her hand. I kiss the back of it tenderly. Neither of us speak. Neither tells the other we love the other. Neither of us gives a heartfelt speech about how we feel in case these are our last moments on this earth. Neither of us has to. For once, we've said the important things. We've shared our feelings. Holding each other's hand with our heads leaning close is all this moment needs.

"Hold on," Nora says, her voice calmer.

The engines roar, the plane speeds up, and we are thundering down the runway. We stop shooting, and I quickly close the door, barely avoiding more incoming bullets.

I turn, looking at Siren, wanting her face to be the last thing I see before I die if this is to be my time.

"We've survived hundreds of gunfights, we've won against countless enemies, you survived a drowning, I survived a crazy madman. We are not going to die in a plane crash, you idiot," she says with more confidence than she should have.

"Sometimes, it's the little things that kill you. It's not often the most dangerous thing that kills you. It's moments like this you let your guard down and aren't prepared to battle death."

"We aren't going to die," Siren says, laughing at my jumping leg.

"We might."

"You'd think that even if we were flying a regular plane. You hate Nora's flying."

"I do."

"We aren't going to crash."

"How do you know?"

"Because we are already in the air, you idiot."

I look past her for the first time, out the window. We are in the air. *Holy fucking cow! We are in the air. We're flying!*

"Woo, hoo! Take that, bad guys!" Nora shouts.

We all applaud her, and Siren jumps up and runs to Nora in the captain's chair.

"You did that! You were incredible! I'm so fucking proud of you," Siren squeezes her tightly.

"Okay, okay," Nora says, pushing Siren off her. "I still have to fly this plane and then land, which isn't going to be an easy task."

"But one you are going to handle amazingly, because you are a fucking badass motherfucker," Siren shouts, squeezing her friend again.

Nora laughs. "Yes, I'll be prepared for landing by the time we get where we are going. Which by the way, where are we going?"

I stand up and lean into the doorway of the cockpit. "As far as this plane will take us."

"Somewhere warm would be nice," Lucy shouts. "Especially, if you are planning on leaving me there again."

"I second that. Somewhere warm," Jayden says.

"How far can we go?" I ask Nora.

Nora takes a second to read the computer screen and fuel gages. "We are flying southeast. We could go all the way to New Zealand with a short fuel stop."

"New Zealand work for you?" I ask Lucy, already knowing the answer.

"Hell, yes! I've always wanted to go to New Zealand. Finally, somewhere I can get on board with," Lucy says.

I laugh.

We all laugh.

Siren grabs my cheeks and plants a kiss firmly on my lips. I lift her up, dragging her back to her seat.

"What are you doing?" Siren asks, as I lean her chair back.

"Taking care of you," I say. "First-aid kit?" I ask Lucy.

She tosses it forward. I catch it in the air and set it on the floor in front of me, as I turn toward Siren.

"Did we find any clothing on board?" I ask as Siren's eyes rake down my body.

"Nope, not yet," Jayden answers.

I stare at Siren with intensity in my eyes. "You are going to have to behave then."

She bites her lip. "And what if I don't want to behave?"

"Then, I'll punish you."

Her lips curl up.

Fuck, I really need to try a different tactic.

"Let me see," I say, looking at the wound on her side.

She moves her hands away from her core. I carefully untie the makeshift bandage and then lift her shirt.

She winces slightly; the ribs can be sensitive. It looks like she broke a couple, and there is a large gash on her side.

"I just broke a couple of ribs. I'll survive. It isn't the first time I've broken them," she says, trying to comfort me.

I fucking hate seeing her in pain, even pain I know she can handle.

"Yea, well, I know how badly it hurts. I first broke my ribs when I was seven in a wrestling match with my friends Enzo and Langston. It hurt to breathe, to think, to move."

"I broke mine when I was five," she says.

I frown, not liking the sound of this. *Did her parents abuse her? Did someone else? How else does a five-year-old girl break her ribs?*

"I thought I could fly, so I climbed to the highest branch I could find and jumped," she laughs at my shocked reaction.

"Are you serious?"

"Yes, it hurt like hell. Way worse than this. We didn't have medical insurance, so I just toughed it out. I stayed in bed a lot and ate lots of ice cream. I survived when I was five; I think I'll survive now."

"I know, but if I could take your pain away, I would. I'd take it all myself," I say, pulling some antiseptic out and gauze. The wound isn't deep enough to need stitches.

"I wouldn't let you," Siren says, taking the antiseptic

from me and dabbing some on a few cuts on my chest she's been eyeing. They're more superficial than her wounds.

I take my time placing the gauze across her ribs, giving me more time to examine her reaction when I touch her wound. She barely reacts, though, knowing I'm trying to prove she's in more pain than she's letting on.

Then I look to her cheek. Another cut marks her beautiful skin. I dab antiseptic on it and move to get a bandaid, but Siren grabs my wrist, stopping me.

"Let it breathe," she says, her voice dropping to a serious tone. I realize she's telling me to let her breathe. Don't stifle her; we will never last if I do.

I nod and stop babying her. I close the first aid kit, shivering under her gaze.

"Stop looking at me like that," I say.

"Like what?"

"Like you want me to fuck you. As much as I'm desperate to, I'm tired of fucking you in a bathroom. Even though this plane is huge, there aren't any other rooms on the plane. I'd rather not give Lucy and Jayden a show."

She smirks. "Fine, then we should talk."

I frown. "About what?"

She swallows, fluttering those beautiful lashes at me. Suddenly I wish I had taken her to the cramped bathroom and fucked her no matter how exhausted we both are.

"Lucy," we both say together.

I nod for her to ask her question, intending to answer her.

"Why are those men after Lucy? Why is Bishop after her?" Siren asks.

I open my eyes to answer her, when I feel Lucy's gaze on me. I turn and meet Lucy's gaze. Lucy is fine with me telling her secret. But when I look at Lucy, I realize I'm not fine with it.

I made a promise to Lucy—to keep her secret. I can trust Siren, she would protect the secret, but the secret is dangerous. We have enough enemies. I won't add any more to Siren's list.

"I can't tell you," I say.

Siren blinks rapidly. "You're shitting me, right?"

"No."

Siren waits, looking at me with trepidation, like I might change my mind. I won't. Not about this. I protect. I protect everyone. That's what I do.

Siren stands. "I thought we were done hiding things from each other. I thought we were done with the lying. I thought we love each other. I thought we were sharing everything. I guess I was wrong."

Siren walks into the cockpit, slamming the door. I wince, my heart heavy. I look back at Lucy, and I know I made the right decision. I have to keep the people I love and the people I protect separate.

17

SIREN

MY ANGER FLOWS through me all thirty hours it takes us to get to New Zealand. I stay in the cockpit the entire time, only ducking out to pee and grab food for Nora and me.

I let the anger pull me into a deep sleep in the seat next to Nora, expecting to dream about how much I hate Zeke for letting me love him. For teasing me with the idea that we could have more, and then taking it all away. We can't have more; this is all we can have.

Sins.

And lies.

No truths.

That's who we are. We commit sin after sin. We murder, steal, torture. Then we lie and lie and lie to each other, hiding who we truly are. I'm not even sure I know who Zeke really is. *What kind of man is he?*

My brain drifts off, and I force Zeke out of my head. I can't think about him. I need sleep. Peaceful, quiet sleep. As soon as I push Zeke out, I leave room for another man to enter...

. . .

"See, I told you he would betray you," Bishop says.

"He didn't betray me. He's just not telling me the truth."

He laughs. "Same difference."

"What do you want?"

"The same thing I've always wanted—you."

I wake up in a sweat, staring at blue sky and gray tarmac in front of me.

We landed.

I look over at Nora. "Sorry. I considered waking you, but I thought it might be better you were asleep while I tried to land this thing."

I nod, looking down at my pajama pants and tank top. I'm covered in blood, sweat, and fear.

The images of Bishop haunt me, the words he never spoke to me linger—I let him in again. Zeke didn't heal me. He didn't get rid of Bishop, he just pushed him to the outskirts of my mind. As long as I was thinking about Zeke, Bishop was gone.

Zeke's still my anchor. I'm still in love with him. He is the only man who can save me from Bishop. And yet, I can't shake the feeling that Zeke is also the one man I need to stay away from in order to keep Bishop from succeeding.

"Are you okay?" Nora asks me.

I smile. "Shouldn't I be asking you that? You just flew a plane you had no training to fly. You took off while men were shooting at us. You are one badass woman, you know that, Nora Taylor?"

She blushes. "I'll add it to my resumé. But you are the one who had the man you love lie to you again."

"He didn't lie."

She raises an eyebrow and crosses her arms.

"Okay, close enough."

She takes my hands. "I may be a badass, but only because I learned from the best. You, Aria Siren Torres, are one badass woman. Don't let him have all the power."

I nod. "Let's go."

We walk out of the cockpit, but everyone has already left.

"Lucy hired a limo to pick us up. She said she was tired of riding in shitty cars. If she was going to die soon, then she wanted to enjoy her life and money," Nora says.

Of course, she did.

I walk down the stairs and climb into the back of the limo where Lucy, Jayden, and Zeke are all waiting. Lucy must have had clothes delivered, because Zeke now has on jeans and a clean shirt.

"There are clothes in the bag for you, Siren," Lucy says.

"What? Are you tired of the high schooler in a horror film look?" I ask.

Lucy just smiles, like she's won. She didn't have to tell Zeke to not spill her secrets to me. He did it on his own.

Does he love her more than me? Maybe. Maybe not. It doesn't matter, because he doesn't trust me enough with the truth.

I dig through the bag and pull out a designer sweatshirt and pull it on, getting it covered in blood and sweat.

Lucy winces.

Even Nora cringes as the expensive fabric becomes saturated.

Zeke's lip twitches, but I don't look at him. *Nope.* Not until he starts talking. I'm holding a silent protest when it comes to him. He won't talk to me, so I won't talk to him.

"Where are we going?" Nora asks.

"The house I bought," Lucy smiles.

"More like a mansion," Jayden says.

"Isn't that inconspicuous? Don't you want to hide somewhere less obvious?" Nora asks.

"Yes, she should," I say.

I feel Zeke's stern glare on me, pleading with me to be nice. I'm tired of being nice. I'll go back to being a bitch. I'm good at it. Nice is overrated anyway. You still end up with the same hurt no matter what.

"The house is secluded, near the ocean. I'd rather have an awesome view and die young, than live the rest of days in a shithole," Lucy answers.

"Plus, she hired a huge security team," Jayden says like it's a good thing.

I want to glance at Zeke so badly. We both know bigger isn't always better. You want a highly *skilled* team. That's all that matters. You need a team that will sacrifice everything for you—a smart person in charge, who can jump quickly between plans and is loyal above everything else.

I have no idea who Lucy hired. Just because she can throw her money around doesn't mean she's being smart about it. If she didn't let them know how important it was to not tell a soul who they were working for, then hiring them is more dangerous than not hiring anyone.

But I'm done helping Lucy. Not without lots of answers first. I'm done.

The limo pulls up in front of a mansion on the beach, just like Lucy said. *Yep, definitely not inconspicuous.* Everyone on the damn island knows we are here now.

We all file out. I make sure to exit after Nora and ignore Zeke completely. As soon as we step out, we are greeted by a large staff asking us if we have bags and if we are hungry.

I glance at Nora since I can't look at Zeke. This is going to end badly for Lucy.

But I catch Zeke drop his head out of the corner of my eye. He feels the same, and it kills him to not be able to protect his friend.

"Lucy, let's talk a minute," I say, not asking, but telling her. I grab her arm and yank her into the house, up the stairs, to what I assume is the master bedroom. If not, it is one hell of a spectacular room.

"What are you doing?" I ask, releasing her arm.

"Living."

"No, you are risking everything. Why?"

Lucy walks to the window and looks out at the ocean. "Because I'm dying. And I'm tired of dying without really living."

"What are you talking about?"

She turns toward me, with a tight smile. "I'm dying, Siren. I have breast cancer. Stage four."

Shit. I want to apologize for every bad thing I've ever said to her. "I'm so sorry."

"Don't. I don't want your sympathy."

I walk to the window where she's standing. "I'm not going to pretend to understand. But I'm here if you need me."

She nods. "I don't need you. I don't need anyone."

"That's not true. Everyone needs someone, especially if—"

"I'm dying. No, I don't need anyone."

"But, Zeke..."

"He would do everything and anything. He would move mountains trying to find doctors to save me. He would sacrifice everything to be with me. I don't want that."

"There has to be someone you want by your side," I say.

"There was, but I broke up with her."

"Her?"

"Yes, I'm bisexual. I fell in love with a woman after Zeke. Maybe no man could ever compare to Zeke, so I never even tried to love a man again. I don't know. No, that isn't true. I just love who I love. And I love Palmer. But I can't be with her in the end. I won't let anyone watch me die."

"Lucy, that's not fair. Does she know?"

"Yes, and she was more than happy to be let off the hook to take care of me," Lucy says.

I take her hand as the tears fall from both of our eyes.

Fuck.

Life isn't fair.

Love isn't fair.

Lucy loved two people in her life. But neither love was enough to last, not even to the end of her short life.

"I can be here, if you want."

Lucy shakes her head. "No, I don't want that. I want my solitude. But I want to die, here, alone. Not suffering. Not letting anyone else see my pain. I want to be pampered and spend my money how I want. I want to live the rest of my days in paradise."

"Whatever you want. I understand," I say.

She nods.

"Can I ask you one thing?" I ask.

"You can ask me whatever you want. It doesn't mean I'll answer."

I smile at that. "Do you still love Zeke?"

Lucy's bottom lip quivers, and she looks down to the beach where Zeke is standing, pensively looking out at the ocean. The ocean is where he belongs. I've never seen him on the ocean when he was whole and not hurt or trying to stay alive, but I know the ocean still calls to him.

"Yes, how could I not love him?"

I suck in a breath. *Love is so not fair.*

"But he loves you more," Lucy continues. "I won't take him away from you. Even when I'm dying. I don't want to take him from you."

"It doesn't matter who he loves more. He protects everyone he loves. And he loves you. His love for you is different than his love for me. Just like his love for Enzo and his family is different. It makes no difference the level of his love. He protects us all the same." I squeeze her hand in reassurance that if she wants Zeke's help, she's got it. No matter what.

Zeke's good at protecting. He just compartmentalizes all of us, keeping us separate. It makes it easier for him to protect us. He never has to choose who deserves to be saved. He just saves us.

"You should tell him. He deserves to know the truth," I say.

"You deserve the truth, too," Lucy says.

I suck in a breath. "Maybe, but he has to be the one to tell me the truth. I want the truth, but only if he's willing to give it. I don't want to hear you tell his truth."

"I know. I wasn't suggesting I tell you what Zeke won't. Just know that he will. He'll open up to you someday, because you're wrong. He doesn't treat us all the same. One day, he'll have to choose. And he'll choose you."

"What do you want me to do?" I ask.

"Tell Zeke you think I'll be safe here. I didn't hire idiots. I had Jayden hire the team—a team he said you would approve of."

"Okay."

"Convince Zeke to leave. To fight like he always does."

"What will you do?"

"I'll live and keep fighting until my dying breath.

Whether it be cancer or a bullet that kills me, it makes no difference."

I nod. "I'll honor your wishes for as long as I can. But if Zeke asks, if he suspects you're sick, I won't lie for you. I'll tell him the truth."

She squeezes my hand. "I'm counting on it."

We both stand, looking out at the ocean with tears in our eyes. *Who knew that we would be like this?* Not friends, but more. We share a connection. We share a love. I don't know how we could get any closer to each other.

The vibration of my phone breaks the beautiful moment.

I walk into the hallway to take the call, letting Lucy have her moment of solitude.

"Yes?" I answer, already knowing who's calling me.

"I want him back here. I have a task for him," Julian says.

I hang up, not answering him. *Shit, shit, shit.*

I slump to the floor as I cry. For Lucy. For Zeke. For me.

Love really isn't fair.

18

ZEKE

I'M SITTING on a wicker chair on one of the six balconies this house has. *Six!* It's ridiculous. It's huge, beautiful, and so Lucy. But that doesn't mean that I understand why she's risking her life to live in this beautiful house. She should hide out for a few weeks and then buy something like this when it's safe.

Nora sits in a wicker chair to my left. Siren sits across from me, not looking at me.

Nora is the first to break the silence. "I called this meeting to discuss our next plans. Siren would like you to know she's interviewed all of the security team and staff, and she thinks this is the best place for Lucy."

"Bullshit," I say, looking at Siren. She doesn't look up at me.

"Siren would also like you to know that Lucy is giving you her bank account to spend as you see fit."

"I'm not taking Lucy's money. I'll tell her that myself," I grumble.

Nora sighs. "Siren would also like you to know that Julian called. He wants her to bring you back."

"What else does Siren want me to know? Does she want to suck my dick? Ready to spread her pretty legs for me? Or is she planning on slitting my throat in my sleep? Tell me, Nora, since you speak for Siren."

Nora frowns. Siren doesn't react.

"Siren would like to discuss how to handle Julian. She thinks it's a good idea to go back. To see what he's up to, and devise a plan to kill him. You have too many enemies right now. It's time to eliminate one."

I growl. "I'm not talking to you through Nora, Siren. That's not what's fucking happening. If you want to talk to me, you talk to me. Understand?"

Siren doesn't react. She doesn't look at me. She doesn't speak.

"I get it. You're pissed I won't tell you the truth. Well, I'm pissed you won't tell me what's up with Lucy. We both know this is the worst place for her to be. Bishop and his men will find her in a heartbeat, and then everything we've been through, losing Dylan, will be for nothing."

Nothing. I get fucking nothing out of her.

"I'll arrange flights back to St. Kitts," Nora says. "Should we fly commercial or private again? I don't mind flying, but I need some rest first."

"Nora, can you give Siren and me a minute alone? As for flights, don't worry about them. We aren't going anywhere until Siren talks to me. She's stubborn, so it could be years before I crack her." I stand up and feel Nora's eyes on me. But Nora's eyes aren't whose I care about. I lean forward and whisper in Siren's ear. "I'm counting on it taking at least a couple hours. Three to be exact. Three hours to break you into talking to me. And I'm going to love every second of it."

Nora leaves, and I grab Siren's hand. She tries to pull away, acting like her hand just touched a hot stove she can't get away from fast enough. Not like it's me, who her body craves to touch, with every part of her being.

I yank her up and sit down on her chair, forcing her down onto my lap. Her hands start fighting against me like I knew they would. There is no passion behind her fighting; she isn't really trying to get me to stop holding her. She just wants to be left alone to stoop and be angry.

Not happening.

"I can't tell you Lucy's secret," I start, hoping she will at least hear my words, and they will spark a fire in her body.

I feel her body heat up, and her core twitch as she sits on my lap, dying to fight me. To hurt me. To show me how much I hurt her by not telling her.

There's my girl. Fight me. Show me you care.

"I can't tell you Lucy's secret because it will put you in danger. If Bishop and his men found out you knew Lucy's secret, they would be after you the same way they're after her. They'll try to torture you to get you to spill the information."

I grab her chin, turning her head to look at me, to see how much I care.

"I'm not hiding the truth from you because I don't trust you. I'm not hiding the truth because I think you will use it to hurt Lucy. I'm not telling you the truth to protect you."

She pushes my hands away, still not putting much energy into the motion.

"I'm sorry, Siren. So fucking sorry," I say, my words filled with all the conflict I feel.

She turns her head, but I snap it back.

"I'm sorry," I say again with everything I have in me. Finally, I see it. I see her break just a little. The hard shell she put up now has a crack in it. I plan on pushing my way through until she lets me all the way in and doesn't let me back out again—ever.

She slaps me.

It stings, but more because it's a surprise move than an actual shock to my face. The redness will leave in less than a minute, the pain I won't feel after a second. It's just not Siren's style. She's not a slapper; she's a puncher.

She doesn't want to fight. She wants to hide away. That's the only way she thinks she can keep her heart safe from me.

After watching a man die, a man who was too young, I'm tired of waiting. I'm tired of not fighting for what I want. And I want Siren—forever.

"I'm sorry," I say again. Then my lips capture hers, tasting their soft deliciousness.

She pulls back and gives my chest a hard shove. She stands, but I grab her wrist, jerking her back to me.

This time, she punches me in the jaw.

I let go of her hand as I see stars for a second, but I can't wipe the smile off my face. She's pissed. That's a good sign. It means I'm winning. It means I'm getting under her skin. It means she still cares.

I move my jaw side to side, trying to loosen the pain, and then I chase after her. She's only made it into the kitchen when I reach her.

"Siren!" I yell, my voice is gravelly and deep. My voice hits her deep and lands right between her legs. I'm not just saying I'm sorry. I'm saying I love you. I want to make it up to you. Let me love you.

She gives me a stern warning to stay away with her tightened eyes and a clenched jaw.

I smile at her reaction. It's exactly what I want. If I can't get her to admit that she still loves me, then I want her to hate me. Her hating me is the same as her loving me. The only difference is that when she hates me, it's only because she's trying to protect herself. She's trying to push me away to protect us both.

Not going to happen. Not again.

I walk over to her. To my surprise, she doesn't run. I figured I'd have to chase her across half the property. But then I see why she's not running. Lucy is standing in the kitchen, fixing herself a peanut butter sandwich.

"Lucy," my voice is a warning.

"Yes?" Lucy answers. One sassy word used to be able to put me on my knees when it came to this woman. I would do whatever she wanted. Not anymore.

I love Lucy, yes. But not like I love Siren. Not anywhere near what I feel for her. Right now, this isn't about Lucy. This is all about Siren.

I walk over to Siren, who is standing next to Lucy. The two women exchange glances, and the look runs deep, to a level of understanding that only women who have been best friends for years typically share. Something happened between the two of them. Something brought them closer, possibly even closer than I am to Lucy.

I don't care about that right now. I only care about Siren. I round the island they are standing at, and box Siren in with my hands. I don't touch her, but it's clear that I'm about to.

She growls. It's the first sound she's made. It's not a word, but it's the first step to her telling me off. I'll take it.

"Lucy, could you give Siren and I some privacy?"

Lucy laughs. "This is my house. You can't order me out of my own kitchen. If you want privacy, go to a bedroom."

"Oh, we will. But not yet," I say, my voice full of threats.

Lucy takes her time finishing the sandwich, which is just

fine with me. It gives me more time to watch Siren sweat. More time for her anger to stew. More time for her to get riled up and ready to fight back.

Finally, Lucy walks over to me, holding the last bite of sandwich in one hand.

"Don't hurt her." She slaps me hard across the face.

"What the hell was that for?" I ask.

Lucy looks from me to Siren. "You fucked up. You deserved to be slapped, although I'm sure Siren can more than make you pay for what you did to her. That's for hurting my friend. Don't do it again."

Then Lucy walks away.

Yea, these two definitely got close, and I don't understand how. I mean, I love them both. I would love them both to be able to be in my life, but the fact that they've become friends so quickly is suspicious.

I eye Siren, but I only get one shot at getting her to talk to me. As much as I'm curious about what brought on their friendship, I care more about getting Siren to talk about us.

"I'm sorry," I say the words again that I know will cut deepest.

Siren shakes her head, trying to keep from being affected. With us, it's impossible not to feel everything the other is feeling.

I grab her hips, pulling her to me. Her hands go on top of mine, her nails dig into them, making it as hard as possible for me to hold onto her body. I don't care about the pain. I care about her. I would hold her close to me, feeling our hips pressed together, even if there were a thousand knives being driven into me at the same time.

"Fight me, Siren. Tell me how wrong I was. Tell me what I did was wrong. Tell me how you hate me for hurting you," I say, taunting her.

She just digs her nails in deeper into my hands, until I suspect she's drawing blood.

I tilt my head, leaning down. "Kiss me."

She shakes her head.

"You know you want to. Kiss me."

She growls.

I grin, moving my lips over hers.

She bites her lip, trying to keep it from me.

"I'm so sorry, Siren. I hate hurting you." I slide my hands up her body, while her hands try to push me down. I kiss her, but she doesn't push me away immediately. She doesn't kiss me back, either. She simply lets me explore her mouth. She lets me massage her tongue with my own. She lets me moan into her mouth.

Quickly, she grabs my balls and tightens her grip so tight I'm afraid she's going to rip them off.

Her eyes raise, challenging me to touch her again and have her rip my balls off.

"Tell me to stop, and I'll stop. Your body is telling me to bend you over the counter right now and fuck you."

She narrows her eyes, calling bullshit.

I smirk, careful not to move because she does have my balls in her fist. As much as I love her down there, I'd prefer her to be more level headed when she's touching me.

"I guarantee if I dipped my hand beneath your panties right now, they'd be wet." I glance down. "Your nipples are peaked on your beautiful breasts."

Her eyes drop, noticing what I can see so clearly beneath her white shirt. "Your lips are plump, pink, and wet, begging me to kiss you. You can hate me. You can be mad at me. Talk to me. Get it all out. Then we can have the best makeup sex of our lives."

She shakes her head.

"No? You don't want to kiss me?"

She releases me, her fire dimming. She's telling me to leave her alone. She doesn't want to talk. Not about us. Only about whatever plan she has to take down Julian.

But I don't give a shit about Julian right now. Not when she's hurting. Not when I'm failing her.

"Fine, you don't want me to kiss you, then I'll leave. I'll make sure Lucy is safe, and then I'll disappear out of your life forever."

I release her, and take a step back, calling her bluff.

I look up the stairs to where Lucy went. *Can I really leave Siren?*

No.

But Siren can't handle me leaving either.

I take a step toward the stairs, and she flings herself at me. Her arms go around my neck, her lips press against mine, and my erection presses hard into her crotch.

The kiss knocks me back, to the opposite side of the kitchen into the counter behind me. I should have taken her to the bedroom. I really miss fucking her in a bed. But I don't think either of us can make it up to the bedroom right now.

Her kisses are hungry and aggressive; she uses her teeth as much as her tongue with every kiss. I give her the sharp points of my teeth right back.

We go bite for bite, nibble for nibble. Drawing the taste of blood on each other's lips.

Our teeth aren't the only thing drawing blood. Our nails claw into each other's backs.

I grab her shirt, ripping it from her body.

She does the same to mine, our shirts flung to the floor and ripped to shreds.

"Don't ever wear a bra again," I say, staring down at her gorgeous breasts.

She responds by biting down on my earlobe.

I push Siren back until her ass is shoved into the counter.

She smirks, goading me on.

"Oh no, my love, I'm about to give you so much more," I say.

I grab her jeans, unbuttoning and unzipping, yanking them down her body. My hand disappears beneath her panties a second later, and just as I knew they would be, they are soaked.

"You can pretend you don't want me all you want, but your body will never lie to me."

There is a storm brewing in her eyes as she grips the counter while my fingers circle her clit. She lets me. She lets herself feel how good it feels.

It doesn't matter that we are in the middle of a kitchen that more than a dozen people could walk into at any moment. Siren may not be talking, but she's groaning loudly enough to send a warning to everyone to stay the fuck away.

As if a timer goes off in her head, Siren only lets herself enjoy the moment for a minute. Then she's grabbing my jeans, shoving them over my hips, and searching for what she needs beneath my boxers. She grabs me roughly, taking all of me in her hand with desperation in her eyes.

We both tease and taunt each other with our hands; our mouths go to work devouring each other. It's not enough, not nearly enough. I need all of her. I need to be inside her. And she needs me there. We both need each other.

I bend her over the counter, her ass in the air, my cock pressing between her legs at her slick entrance. Her body is so damn ready for me. If only her mind and heart would get there just as fast. I push, but she pushes back.

"Enough," she says, turning and pushing me from her body.

We are both standing bare naked in the kitchen in front of each other. Panting, wet, and smelling like the sex we never finished. Both bleeding from our lips and back. Both bruised from where our hands touched each other too hard.

I want to fuck her. Make love to her. But I got her to speak. And her words are what I needed more.

I'm quiet, begging her to talk.

"You hurt me, Zeke. I'm tired of being hurt. You aren't the only one hiding a secret. I'm hiding secrets too. And I hate it!" Her voice breaks, her bottom lip trembles, and a tear drips from the corner of her eye.

"I'm tired of hiding every truth. Even if I'm doing it to protect you. I'm tired of carrying that burden alone. I'm so tired, Zeke."

Dammit.

"I love you isn't enough. Choosing me over everyone isn't enough. We will always have to hide the truth. Hurt each other. Go it alone in order to protect each other." Siren takes a step toward me. Each step is strengthening her as she finds her voice. Her words. Her truth.

"What are we doing together, Zeke? Loving each other isn't enough. We will never settle down. We will never get married. We will never have kids."

My heart clenches. *Damn, do I want all those things with her.* I want to get down on one knee right now and propose with the biggest ring I can find. But how can two people be married when all they do is lie and hide the truth? Even if we could find a way, I don't have a dime to buy even the smallest of rings.

"It's a sin to keep the truth from you, a man I wish was my husband. And yet, I have to keep committing the sin over and over. And you have to do the same."

She grips her stomach. "Jesus, what I wouldn't give to have your baby inside me. To be growing a life you and I started. But we can never even discuss the topic because of the lives we chose."

I stare at her bare beautiful stomach, trying to imagine how incredible it would be to see her round and plump, my baby inside her. I can't think of anything better. *But how could we bring a baby into this world of danger?* I can barely keep Siren safe. *How could I keep a baby safe?*

"Our love story will end tragically. We should just end it now. End it before it really starts. End it before we hurt each other more than we already have," she says.

I hold her tear-stricken cheeks in my hands, rubbing the tears with my thumbs. Finally, I find my voice to help her understand what's inside of me.

"I don't know how our story ends. I don't know if I can propose marriage. I don't know about filling a house with babies. But I do know this—our love story will be the most powerful and epic of all time. We make sacrifices for the other no one else has to make for love. We are willing to give it all up—the chance to be married, have kids, live happily ever. We are willing to go through all the pain to love each other, however short it is. It all tells me that we love each other more than two people have ever loved each other. It tells me that our love story is going to be epic."

19

SIREN

How could I ever give up this man?

This man would give up everything for me. This man is torn up inside at having to keep truths from me, but willing to carry that burden forever, because he loves me, and he can't stand to hurt me.

Most people wouldn't understand our love. Most wouldn't understand how what we are doing is love. But, I don't give a fuck about other people. This is our love story, dammit, even if we have to hide everything from each other —every truth, every lie, every sin. We will do it for love. We will fight for love. We will fight for someday in the future to be able to spill every truth we've ever learned.

"Sin," I say.

"What?"

"Sin. I can't tell you the truth. And neither can you. I think it's time to commit a sin."

"Oh, yea?" His brow raises.

"Yea."

He grabs me and throws me over his shoulder. He

carries me up the stairs, heading into the first bedroom he can find.

We fall onto the bed together, naked, his cock settling between my thighs, and our mouths pressing against each other in broken kisses.

I feel his tip push at my entrance.

"Zeke," I say, pushing his lips back. My voice is soft and full of emotion.

"Yes?" he asks, his voice strained, trying to keep it together before he can take me in this bed.

"I haven't taken the pill. I left it in Lithuania," I say.

"Fuck," he curses. He looks around the room, begging to find a condom somewhere. He crawls up my body and reaches into the nightstand drawers, throwing each drawer open and slamming it shut in frustration when he doesn't find what he's looking for.

He takes a deep breath and then moves back onto his forearms, resting around my head as his cock still sits waiting impatiently at my entrance.

"Do you trust me?" he asks calmly.

I don't know what he's asking. *Do I trust him to take care of a baby if he gets me pregnant? Do I trust that he won't come inside me? What?*

"God, does it even matter? I just need you," I say, grabbing his hair and yanking his lips back down on my body.

He slides in as I greedily kiss his lips like I haven't kissed him in months.

In and out Zeke slides. Our bodies already so familiar with each other that we know exactly what the other wants. Desires. Needs.

I shift my hips as his hand glides under my ass, holding me up so he can drive deeper inside me.

My lips open wider, begging his tongue to come in deeper.

I need more.

Deeper.

Harder.

All of him.

He can't get deep enough inside me either.

"I can't promise you a traditional marriage," Zeke says, thrusting.

"I can't promise you the large diamond ring you deserve."

He pulls out, then pushes all the way in, filling me completely just like his words.

"I can't promise you, babies."

He kisses me as his body pushes me deeper, harder, longer.

"But I can promise you forever. I can promise to love you, to protect you with everything I have. Over everyone else in my life. You're first. You're it. You're everything. And I'll do everything in my power to make the ring, the wedding, the babies come true if that's what you want. I want everything for you, everything."

I don't want him to put me first. I don't want him to ever have to choose me over someone else he loves. Hopefully, it will never come to that. If it does, I won't let him keep that promise.

For now, it's what I need to hear.

"I promise you the same," I say.

"I love you."

"I love you, too."

All the built-up anger, frustration, and pain takes over at the same time that all the love, happiness, and joy hit me. It makes for one explosive orgasm.

Zeke pulls out and his cum coats my stomach. He collapses on top of me, not giving a damn that he's smearing his cum all over both of our bodies. We can't part yet. We need to stay connected.

Connected—it's how we fall asleep.

"Do you have it yet?" Bishop asks.

"Have what?"

He growls. "Lucy's weapon."

"What? Lucy's what?"

"Zeke knows. You need to get it from him, before someone else does."

I wake up in a sweat. From the nightmare or the big brute of a man on top of me.

I can't control my breathing. My tears. My voice.

Zeke wakes up instantly. He rolls off of me but pulls me close as he grabs a gun, assuming I'm worked up because there is a threat in the room. There is none.

When he realizes we're physically safe, he drops the gun and looks at me. He cups my face in his hand.

"Baby, I got you. It was just a nightmare. I got you; you're safe."

Safe.

There is no such thing as safe in my world.

Zeke rocks me in his arms, like I'm a child waking up needing to be coaxed back to sleep.

After several minutes pass, he asks, "Bishop?"

I don't answer. He already knows. I hate that he failed. That he didn't take the nightmares away. That I'm still in this pain. Still terrorized by a man whose actions I can't even remember.

"I'm scared," I say instead.

"Me too."

"We have too many enemies. We can't keep fighting from three different angles. It's too much."

Zeke nods. "Who do we go after first?"

"Julian Reed."

Zeke takes a deep breath and kisses my temple. "I agree."

"We need more people on our side. We're not—"

"We are plenty strong enough. But I agree, it's time to bring more people to our side."

"How? Who?"

"Let me worry about that. For now, we need to go face Julian. And we need to draw Bishop away from Lucy."

We are going to take down Julian Reed. I never thought the day would come. I never thought I'd be free. I'm still not sure it can be done, or if it's the right move.

I don't know who Julian is working with, where he got his money, or how many enemies we are going to make by taking him down. But I'm tired of living in fear. We are going to do this—together. Our love is strong enough to take down any enemy. Even the devil.

20

ZEKE

WE DRIVE from the airport straight to Julian's. We have a plan. And a plan after that one and another plan after that one. We won't stop until he's dead. Not this time.

Julian Reed has too much power. Too much money. We have to eliminate him.

I stop my truck in front of Julian's house. We both climb out silently, and then I take Siren's hand as we walk into the house without knocking.

We are tired of pretending we don't care about each other. Tired of pretending that Siren is loyal to Julian. She isn't. I don't care what Julian is holding over her; we are about to end it.

"Remember, we have one shot. We have to do this now. We can't—" Siren says.

I turn to her, kissing her on the lips. "I know. We won't fail."

I won't fail. I will do whatever it takes to free her of Julian. And then I'll keep fighting until all of our enemies are dead. Until she is safe.

Of all our enemies, I don't know which man scares me the most.

Julian scares me because she's worked for him for so long. He's wealthy. And he's hiding too much shit.

Bishop scares me because somehow he got into her head and fucked it up. We both still don't know what he did and didn't do to her.

We walk into Julian's office. Siren texted him earlier today, so he should be expecting us. We find the whole house empty, except for a crackling conference speaker on Julian's desk. Julian's voice greets us as we enter his office.

"Oh, look at that. How sweet? Walking in here like you are on the same side. Like she's yours," Julian says. He must be watching us from the cameras on the ceiling.

"It's over, Julian. I'm not yours anymore. I never was. You're not even here to face me, you coward," Siren says.

"Hmm, I'm sure you believe that, Aria, but you've figured out how to lie now, so I'm not sure."

"I can't lie," she says.

Julian laughs. "You just did. Even if I were there in person, you wouldn't kill me," Julian says.

"You have no idea what I'm capable of, Julian," I threaten.

"I know how to stop Bishop from being in her head," he says.

Fuck...

"As I was saying, we are on round three of our little game. Keep playing, and I'll tell you how to rid Siren of Bishop. Truth or sin?"

"Sin," I say wearily.

"Get me a yacht."

I frown.

"Not just any yacht. The best," Julian says.

Fuck, he means an Enzo Black yacht. One of the yachts belonging to my best friend and former boss.

I pound my fist on the desk next to the speaker. "And when I bring you your damn yacht, you will tell me how to stop the voices in her head."

"When you finish all five rounds, I'll tell you."

"No, after this round."

"When you finish all five rounds, I'll tell you."

Goddammit.

I grab Siren's arm and pull her out of the room, desperate to finish this. Desperate to save her from all of our enemies. Desperate to ring Julian's neck with my bare hands. Desperate to keep the love I just found.

21

SIREN

I punch Zeke in the shoulder, but it barely moves him as we step outside of Julian's house.

"Ow, what was that for?" Zeke grumbles, rubbing his bicep like I just shot him there.

I roll my eyes. "You know exactly what that was for. You didn't even fight. You didn't even try. That was our chance! Our chance to take down Julian Reed forever," my lip trembles as I speak, and my voice drops out.

I blink rapidly as my brain becomes overtaken by men. So many damn men in my head.

Kill him, Bishop says.

You will never get free, Julian says.

You're mine, Zeke says.

"Stop!" I yell, squeezing my head, trying to get the fucking voices to stop.

"Siren, baby, take a deep breath. I got you."

I hear Zeke's words, but I don't register them. I'm lost to the fog that is my brain. The voices are going to haunt me forever. Long after the men are gone, the voices are still going to be with me. Threatening me. Telling me what to do. Trying to control me.

I fall to my knees, shaking viciously. "Get out of my head!"

Zeke holds me, for a long time. We just sit on the driveway in front of Zeke's truck. It isn't safe here. We shouldn't stay at Julian's for a second longer than we need to. But neither of us care.

I need Zeke to hold me. I need to feel safe. I need to feel protected, even if I'm not. Bishop fucked with my head. His voice was one too many. It was bad enough to hear them when I was dreaming, but now I hear them everywhere I go.

Finally, I stop shaking, and Zeke lifts me up and puts me in the truck. Then he climbs into the driver's seat and drives us away.

"This is why I made the deal. You can't live like this. You need help. We need help. Doctors aren't going to be enough to save you," Zeke says.

I frown. Hating that he's right, but he is. He's fucking right. Whatever Bishop did to me goes beyond normal medicine.

"I'm going crazy," I say.

Zeke takes my hand in his large palm and kisses the back of my hand. "You're not crazy. But I don't want you alone. Not anymore. Promise me?"

I nod.

I shake my head, like that will somehow clear my thoughts of the voices. *Just start talking, think about something else, that will help.*

"Where are we going?" I ask.

"To the airport. And then, Miami."

"Miami?"

Zeke nods slowly.

"Are we going to meet..." I can't finish the sentence; I'm in too much shock.

"Yes, I'm taking you to meet my family," Zeke says, referring to his former boss, his friends, his life before I saved him.

I suck in a breath. I've wanted nothing more for months now, ever since I saved Zeke, and Julian put me to task to learn who Enzo Black is. I've wanted nothing more since I fell in love with Zeke and wanted to learn and know everyone he loves. Zeke has already met everyone in my life. It's pathetic, but I only have one true friend. A dead ex-husband. Dead parents. And a sociopath trying to control my life.

Zeke may have also come from the underground, criminal world, but he had friends, family, a life he loved. I don't know much about Zeke. I don't know what kind of house he would choose to live in. I don't know his favorite foods or movies. I don't know if he prefers pop or rap or hip-hop music. Or if he's a secret country music lover. I don't know anything about his life before. Not really. I know he's good with a gun. I know he protects his people with his life. But I don't know what he loved outside of people.

"Hey," Zeke says softly, his finger slipping under my chin to look up at him.

"You have nothing to worry about. They are going to love you," Zeke says.

I pick at my nails. "I'm worried about Julian or Bishop or someone following. I hate that I'm the reason you have enemies. And we're bringing our enemies to them."

Zeke nods. "I know. I feel like I failed. But we are out of options. We both agree we need help. This is how we get it. These are the best people I know. They are strong and smart. We will win. Trust me."

Zeke looks out the windshield again. "Nora can't come with. I don't want more people involved than need to be."

"I agree. If she knows about your friends, then Julian could torture her. I don't want that."

"Good."

I exhale an exhausted breath. "Maybe I shouldn't come either."

Zeke's eyes go to me like a moth to a flame, not caring about the road in front of him. "Why?"

"Because I've fucked up. I've hurt you. You shouldn't trust me."

"Are you going to betray my friends to Julian?"

"Only if I have to in order to save your life," I answer honestly. The only way I would ever betray his friends would be to save him.

He looks at me with disappointment in his gorgeous dark eyes. He runs his hand through his hair, full of desperation. "You can't do that, Siren. You have to protect them. Put them ahead of me."

"I can't. That's why I should stay."

Zeke considers for a second. "I can't leave you."

"Why?"

"Because Julian or Bishop will come. They will kidnap you. They will..." Zeke looks at me, and I see the moisture in his eyes, I see his knuckles turn white as he grips the steering wheel, I see the vein in his neck bulge, and I see his face redden.

"Promise me you will consider all the options before you ever hurt my friends. Everything you can think of if you have to choose between them and me. Promise me you will try, as if they were your own friends."

I take his hand gently in my hand and stroke his arm, trying to calm him down. "Of course, Zeke. If I ever have to choose, I'll protect them with my life. But if it comes to saving you or protecting someone else, I will always choose you. I love you."

"I love you too," he says. We drive the rest of the way to the airport in silence. We fly in silence. The silence gives me too much time to think.

A voice in my head says, *"He never said he'd choose you over everyone else. If it comes down to you and them, he'll pick them."*

For once, that voice wasn't Julian's or Bishop's or Zeke's. That voice was mine.

———

I have butterflies in my stomach. Enormous, giant winged butterflies that have migrated from my stomach to my chest and throat. I can't ever remember being so nervous before. I don't get nervous.

I'm unshakable. I'm strong. I fight back. But right now, I'm anxious, nervous, all the stress-inducing words.

We're riding in the back of a cab headed to meet Zeke's family. Not his blood family—those people deserted him years ago. Just like me, he's an orphan. But unlike me, he has more than one person in the world who cares about him.

The cab makes a stop in front of a popular pier lined with boat after boat. Most are huge yachts. *Holy shit*, I think, staring up at the giant things. I've been around boats. I've borrowed plenty of Julian's living on the island. But I've never seen anything as impressive as this.

"Ready?" Zeke asks.

I nod, knowing I won't be able to speak, so I don't even try.

We both climb out after I pay for the cab. Lucy put

money into Zeke's account after a long fight between the two of them, but he won't spend it unless it's an emergency. Although, he winces when he watches me pay, hating that he's making me spend my money.

"I'll get a job. I'll wait tables, tend bar, something—"

"Zeke, I have a million dollars in my bank account. I can afford to pay for a cab ride. I understand why you don't want to spend Lucy's money. And no, you aren't working as a waiter. We are going to take out our enemies, and then you can return to whatever life you want. Whatever you did to earn your millions before."

"You mean killing people?"

Now I wince. I sigh. We have a lot to talk about.

Right now, neither of us can think about our future. All we can think about is today. All we can do is focus on survival. Once we survive, then we can figure out our shit. Then we can pay for all the sins we have both committed and decide if that is still the life we want.

Zeke takes my hand silently.

We walk down the pier, past boat after boat, yacht after yacht. He turns left then right, zigging through the maze of boats, apparently knowing exactly where we are going.

"Did you call Mr. Black to let him know we are coming?" I ask, my voice catching in my throat.

Zeke stops abruptly. "Did you just call Enzo Mr. Black?"

"Um...yea?"

Zeke laughs and then kisses my forehead sweetly. "Stop being nervous. You have nothing to be nervous about. And don't call Enzo Mr. Black. He's family."

Family. These people are part of Zeke's family. Unlike me. *What am I?*

His lover?

His girlfriend?

His almost fiancée?

The woman who betrayed him?

We've never put a label on it. Suddenly, my heart is fluttering, my world is spinning, and I have no idea how to make it stop.

We keep walking, until finally, Zeke stops. I feel his pulse in his hand. I look up. He's biting his bottom lip and running his other hand through his hair. It never occurred to me that Zeke would be nervous.

Other than a possible brief encounter before, he hasn't seen them in months. I don't know if he's scared they will be angry at him for making them believe he was dead all this time or what.

But I squeeze his hand, doing my best to reassure him.

And then Zeke jumps onto the yacht. He motions with his head for me to follow. There is a ramp a few feet down, but fuck that.

I jump over just as Zeke did. The exhilaration of jumping tampers the anxiety in my chest.

Zeke winks at me with a smile, and my heart melts. *How did I get a guy like him to fall for me?* I would experience everything dark in my life again just to have a moment where he loves me.

"Stingray," Zeke says the word like a prayer. Like he doesn't believe his own eyes, if this moment is real. The tears in his eyes are real.

I follow Zeke's gaze, not having a clue who stingray is. I gasp when I see her.

The woman I saw before in the ballroom. She's here, and she's just as beautiful as before. She's in dark jeans and a gray shirt that forms over her flat stomach and breasts. Her hair is almost jet-black, shiny, and straight. She has it tied back in a red bandana. The most captivating thing about her is her eyes. They are a piercing green-blue color, like the ocean. She belongs to the ocean.

Zeke quickly lets go of my hand, like he's completely forgotten I was here. The two run to each other.

I've seen Zeke's reunion with a long-lost love before. I saw him greet Lucy and that was painful. But it was nothing compared to this reunion.

This reunion is giving me all the feels. Jealousy at seeing Zeke wrap his arms around this woman in a hug tighter than any he's ever given me. Rage at his cute nickname for her, while me, he still calls Siren to remind himself of what I've done to him. Pain at seeing the tears flow down the woman's cheeks as she holds onto his neck like she can't bear to ever let him go. And love—so much damn love as they hold each other like lovers who just survived a war.

Unlike when I watched Lucy interact with Zeke for the first time, this is different. With Lucy, it was like two lovers and friends catching up, but with Zeke and this woman, it's like they are both part of the same soul that has been split between two bodies and is finally reconnected again.

I've never seen anything so beautiful. I've never seen such love between two people before that doesn't feel anything like romance. They aren't kissing. Their hands aren't moving up and down each other's bodies, trying to cop a feel. All they want is the hug—the closeness. The connection they've both been missing for so damn long.

Zeke pulls back so he can look into her eyes. "I'm so sorry," he says through his tears.

"You have nothing to be sorry for," she says through her own tears.

"For letting you think I was dead. For only telling you that I was alive and not letting you tell anyone else. For not running to you that night in the ballroom. I was too scared of bringing danger into your life again, but I'm afraid I did just that."

The woman holds his hand. I stare at the connection. Not romantic, not like what Zeke and I have. But something just as strong. Surprisingly, I don't feel jealousy over the connection, although I don't understand why.

A voice behind me startles me. "I don't understand it either. Sometimes I think his connection to her is stronger than mine, and I'm married to her. I've died for her. But I don't feel jealous when I see them together. All I feel is love."

I stare at him, realizing he must be Enzo Black. The woman is his wife.

I nod. "Love is more than just romance. It just is."

"I would never deny her love by any man, least of all him," Enzo says.

Our voices carry, getting their attention. This reunion just got bigger.

22

KAI

Zeke's alive.

He's here.

My heart is whole.

I didn't realize until I had him back in my arms again how much I was hurting, how broken I truly was.

I knew Zeke was alive.

I'd even seen it with my own eyes.

But this...this is what I needed.

I needed him back.

In my life, permanently.

I don't care what enemies are following him. I don't care why he left us for over a year. *He's back.*

And no matter what, I'm not letting him go again.

I love him. I'm not in love with him. I have a perfectly incredible husband. But Zeke is part of my soul. When he called me stingray, the nickname that everyone who knows me has adapted because of him, I lost myself. At the same time, I found myself. I became whole.

I will do everything in my power to keep my heart full. I

don't let people I love go. Zeke's here. I'm ready to fight for him.

I spot the woman behind him. A woman who I hope loves him as much, if not more, than I do. Zeke deserves that kind of love. And I won't let him settle for anything less.

23

ENZO

Zeke's alive.

I have no fucking idea how.

How the hell did he survive getting shot and falling into the middle of the fucking ocean?

Not a clue.

But he's here.

Standing on my boat.

Hugging my beautiful wife, who has so many tears in her eyes. Tears she cries for him and only him. A love between them I will never understand.

I let them have their moment. But that moment seems to last forever.

Then I see I'm not the only one watching the exchange. A woman stands a few feet in front of me, staring with heartache in her eyes.

This woman loves Zeke. I'm not sure if she understands their connection isn't a romantic one. If it was, Zeke really would be dead. But when I approach and see this woman's tears up close, I realize she can see what their connection really is, the same as me.

So I speak, reassuring her that she's right, while I try to make sense of what I'm seeing. *I didn't stay up too late last night with the twins, did I?* This is really happening, Zeke is really here.

Then my wife, Kai, spots me. She winks at me.

"Bastard," I curse under my breath.

The woman looks up at me questioningly, but I don't answer her.

My wife knew. Kai knew Zeke was alive this whole damn time. She's known and kept the secret to herself. I'm going to kill them both.

But first, I want a damn hug from one of my best friends who I thought was dead for over a year.

I clear my throat. "Get a room."

Zeke turns. "Jesus fucking christ."

I don't know who moves toward who, but I'm in his arms, being lifted up in the air. I'm a big man, but I have nothing on Zeke. Zeke is a monster of muscles. I'm just ripped.

Zeke is one of the only men I could fight one and one without weapons and probably lose to. I'm man enough to admit it, though.

"You're alive," I whisper, as I find I'm choked up.

"Clearly," Zeke tries to joke with me, but it doesn't work. I'm bawling worse than my twins.

Zeke puts me down, and I pull him into a normal hug, full of tears and pain and open wounds.

"You bastard," I finally say, hitting him hard on the back. "If you're alive, you're supposed to let a man know. Not make me think you're dead for over a year."

"I did let someone know," Zeke winks at Kai, and grips her hand again.

I sigh, knowing I won't be getting any alone time with

my wife for days while these two catch up like chatty women. But I'm smiling. It's been a long time since I've seen Kai smile like this—truly letting her smile reach her eyes. Now that Zeke is back, she will be smiling a lot more.

All of our tears finally stop, enough for Zeke to realize he's been an idiot and hasn't introduced us to the woman he brought with him.

Zeke smiles brightly, though, like he didn't just fuck up. He's a guy and doesn't see that he's hurt the girl a little bit by taking so long to introduce us to her. But his damn smile is infectious, and even the woman is smiling as she walks over to us.

"That was some reunion," she says, wiping her eyes with a nervous grin.

I study the woman closer now, trying to make an initial assessment before Zeke or her say anything.

The woman is beautiful in a mysterious, take no bullshit kind of way. She reminds me of Kai in that sense. She's thin, tall, and her muscles are visible beneath her shirt. Her hair is lighter than Kai's, but just as long.

Zeke reaches out, grabbing her hand so he can pull her to him. Then I see it—the gun at her back.

I raise my brows at Zeke, asking about the gun. *Did he teach her like he taught Kai?*

He smirks, declaring that question ridiculous.

Interesting.

This woman is a fighter. She grew up in this world. She might be more like me than my wife, after all.

"Let me make some introductions," Zeke starts. "This is Kai Miller, also known as Stingray. She's—"

"Actually, it's Kai Black," I interrupt. "But continue."

Zeke grabs Kai's hand, finding the ring and the scrunchie she often wears to remember him.

"Sorry, this is Kai Black," Zeke says, not surprised at all that we are married. "Kai is one of my best friends in the whole world. Kai, this is..." Zeke hesitates for a second, looking down at the woman.

The woman just snickers. "Really? You're going to look to me to give you the answer?"

Zeke laughs at her snarky words. I like her already. Although, I have no idea why he hesitated when saying her name. Maybe he doesn't know how to introduce her to us. They haven't had *the talk* yet.

"Kai, this is Siren Aria Torres. But I just call her Siren. Siren is my girlfriend by title, but so much more belongs to her. She's the love of my life, my everything, my forever. She's the only woman I can ever imagine as my wife, mother of my kids, etcetera, etcetera. She's everything I ever wanted. And I'm completely embarrassing her right now, but I don't care," Zeke leans down and kisses a blushing Siren on the cheek.

Siren holds out her hand to Kai.

Kai takes it and pulls her into a hug. It instantly feels like they just became sisters.

Zeke and I look away, giving the two a private moment.

"I'm so glad he found you. I was afraid I was going to be the love of his life forever, and that just won't do," Kai says.

"I'm glad he has you. Trust me, he's needed you. I'm not always the best thing for him," Siren answers.

Kai chuckles. "I'm not either. But Zeke's life would be boring if he had perfect women in his life."

Dammit, I have a tear in my eye again. I wipe it quickly.

"Now that the hard introduction is out of the way, Siren, this is Enzo Black. My best friend since birth, boss, and all-around reason I am the man I am," Zeke says.

I hug Siren. It feels like the right thing to do even though I'm not much of a hugger.

"It's so nice to meet Zeke's family," Siren says.

"It's nice to meet the woman he loves," I answer.

She nods in agreement. Zeke pulls her to him, wrapping his arms around her chest protectively. It's such a weird thing to see. I've known Zeke all my life, but I've never seen him in a serious relationship. Sure, he's brought women around, but not very often, and never in a relationship kind of way.

If he ever had a girlfriend, he never told me. I don't know what he's been up to this last year, but he's happy. He's in love. And that makes me happy.

"Where is Langston? Liesel?" Zeke asks, looking for them both.

Kai and I both frown, exchanging glances.

"We have a lot to talk about," Kai says.

Zeke nods. "Us too."

Zeke thinks a moment. "Can we take the yacht out for a few hours? I think that would be the safest way to talk."

We all nod in agreement. As much as I'm glad that Zeke is back, I'm going to kick his ass for bringing danger to my doorstep.

24

ZEKE

I DON'T FEEL like I'm ever going to stop crying or smiling. Or laughing or hugging. Or jumping for fucking joy.

This day seemed like it would never come. I thought I'd never see my friends, my family in every sense of the word, again. When I was floating in the water, about to drown, I thought that was it. I thought my life was over. I thought I was dead.

Even when Siren saved me, I thought I'd never survive to see them. And then I did survive, but I thought I would never get rid of the danger in order to go to them. But I have no choice, not anymore.

I grip Siren's hand. I'm too afraid of what Bishop did to her. He fucked with her head. I don't know what his endgame is. *How far did he go? How much control does he have?*

I have to save her. I can't live without her. And I know now, seeing Kai and Enzo again, that they are strong enough to fight. Of course, they welcomed any woman I love in with open arms. Siren is now part of the family, and they will do anything and everything to protect her.

"Come on, let's get this boat somewhere safe," Enzo says,

patting me on the shoulder like he still can't believe I'm here.

I can't believe it either.

"You do remember how to do your job, right? Because I expect you to get back to work ASAP," Enzo teases.

"Absolutely," I say. *God, would I love to be back in this world.* As much as I want that right now, I can't stay. I just need their help. I'll minimize the risk to them as much as I can.

"Hey now, who's the real boss around here?" Kai's eyes light up.

I laugh, knowing full well these two can fight all they want about who is in charge. In the company or in their relationship, they are complete equals. That's why the relationship and company work so well.

Siren's eyes light up watching them. She's mesmerized when she sees Enzo pinch Kai's ass, then dip her before she pinches him right back, and they skip off to float us away from land.

"I like them. Why again haven't you introduced us before?" Siren asks.

I grin. "Help me with the ropes."

We both undo the ropes keeping us tied to the dock, and then I lift up the ramp. I guide Siren to the front of the yacht, put her in front of me, and glide my hands down to her hips, holding her back against my front as we move away from the Miami shoreline and out into the ocean.

"Welcome to my world," I whisper in her ear.

"It's heaven," she says back.

"I know. I could live on a yacht forever. I basically did when I worked for Enzo."

"I never want to leave," Siren says, and I'm not sure if she means the yacht or my arms as she pulls me around her waist.

I rest my head on her shoulder. *I never want to leave either.*

"Hey, lovebirds. I made Italian food and got out the good wine. You in?" Enzo shouts, leaning against the doorway that leads inside to what I know is the kitchen area.

"Can we eat out here?" Siren asks, looking hopeful as the sun sets.

"Where else would we eat?" Enzo smiles back.

"This is one of the most incredible boats I've ever been on," Siren says. Enzo heads back inside to start bringing out the food and wine. It's just us, no cooks, or other employees on board. That's what's safest.

Siren runs her hands over the railing, amazed at the incredible piece of machinery.

I laugh. "It's pretty impressive, isn't it?"

I wiggle my eyebrows when she looks at me, and I glance down to my growing erection.

She just rolls her eyes at me.

"No sex jokes," Enzo says sternly as he carries out two large platters of food.

"Yea, because we aren't ever class on this boat," Kai says, carrying wine glasses and a bottle of wine under her arm. She leans over to Siren. "It's nice having another woman on the boat. I usually hang out with a dozen men. I've tried to hire more women, but I've found that most women don't want to be away from their families for months at end if we have to be out at sea."

Siren smiles. "Here, let me help you." Siren takes the wine glasses from Kai and sets them on the table. We all take a seat, while Kai pours us glasses. Enzo dishes out the pasta meal he made.

"So catch me up. Where is everyone?" I ask, taking a big bite of the pasta.

Kai and Enzo exchange a look, but Kai is the one who starts talking first. "Beckett is out on a mission. The man you met before."

Enzo stops shoveling food in his mouth and stares back and forth between us. "Wait...Beckett knew you were alive?"

I nod.

Kai nods.

Even Siren nods.

"That fucking cunt," Enzo says. "Why didn't he tell me?"

"Because I told him not to," Kai says, at the same time I do.

We smile at each other. It feels so good to be here.

"How long have you known?" Enzo asks, staring at Kai.

"Zeke sent me a letter," Kai says.

Enzo shakes his head in frustration. "And you couldn't tell me?"

Kai looks at him in warning. "I'm sorry, but he was trying to protect us all. Do you blame him for trying to keep us safe?" She raises a brow at him.

"No." Enzo turns toward me. "Thanks for keeping the danger away as long as you could."

"In the spirit of full disclosure, I also saw him when I was in Paris a few weeks ago."

"What? Why didn't you tell me then?" Enzo asks.

Kai and I exchange glances, and I attempt to explain. "We didn't even talk. We just saw each other from across the room. We were there on separate missions. It wasn't the right time, and I still thought I could protect you from all of this."

Kai tears up. "You have no idea how hard it was for me to

not come squeeze you and bring me home with you. No idea."

Dammit, and now we are all crying again. Even Siren and Enzo are dabbing at their eyes.

"What changed?" Enzo asks softly.

My eyes cut to Siren, who has stiffened next to me.

Enzo's eyes follow, and he knows why—Siren. Siren happened.

"Where are Langston and Liesel? Fighting somewhere or fucking?" I ask, laughing at our old running joke about the two of them.

Enzo picks up his wine glass, avoiding answering.

Kai drops her fork.

The clink of the fork on the plate is the only sound for a second.

"Liesel wanted some space. We actually don't know where she is at the moment. Last time we heard from her she was in Hawaii," Kai says.

"And Langston took off. He couldn't stand that Liesel didn't want to be with him, so he's been getting over her on safaris and expeditions. He's hard to get a hold of, because he's always in some remote location," Enzo explains.

My mouth gapes at them. Enzo, Langston, and I were like the three musketeers. We did everything together. I was as close, if not closer, to Langston than I was Enzo.

And Liesel was always around. When I left, the tension between Langston and Liesel was high. I thought for sure the two would end up together.

"I'll make sure to contact Langston and let him know you are alive. He needs to know. I thought about telling him sooner, but he needed space, and I wanted to honor your wishes," Kai says.

I nod, but the awkward air continues. There was a lot I

missed while I was gone. Just like there is a lot they have missed.

We all finish eating. Enzo clears our plates. And then we drink our wine while the sun sets.

"I guess it's my turn to explain everything," I say.

All eyes are on me, as I explain everything. How Siren saved me. The dangers we are both in from Julian and Bishop. The nightmares Siren has been having.

I wait for Enzo to get pissed at me for bringing the danger to their doorstep, but he doesn't.

"I think we are going to need more wine," he says, getting up and fetching another bottle. He returns and fills all our glasses.

"Zeke didn't tell you everything, though. I hurt him. I—" Siren starts.

"I told them everything that matters," I say, cutting her off. I don't want her to talk about how she hurt me. How she betrayed me. I can forgive her, but I'm not sure they will.

Siren frowns, but Kai just smiles behind her wine glass. Enzo looks completely bewildered by what is happening.

"I'm sorry, I failed you all. I brought danger to your doorstep, when I shouldn't have. But I didn't have a choice... I..." I can't bring myself to talk to them about Siren with her sitting next to me.

She wouldn't let me anyway. She'd get frustrated that the only reason we are sitting here, the only reason we are risking my friends' lives is because of her. "We shouldn't have come here, but—"

"Yes, you should have," Kai says, once again with tears in her eyes.

"You should have come here first thing. You should have told us as soon as you healed and got to that island alive, you asswipe," Enzo says, cursing at me to keep from crying again.

His phone buzzes, and he looks down with a smile staring at the screen.

"The twins are up," he says, exchanging a glance with Kai.

He stands up but studies my face waiting for it to hit me. It does three seconds later.

"Wait. What? Twins? Please tell me he's talking about babies and not some hot blondes he has stashed away in a prison on this boat."

Enzo winks at me, "I'll be right back."

Kai can't stop smiling at me, and I can't stop smiling at her. But I don't speak, and neither does she. We wait for Enzo to return before she explains what the hell is going on. I imagine it's the most incredible thing possible.

Siren is chewing on her bottom lip nervously.

I glance over and whisper to her. "You okay?"

She nods, not telling me what she's worried about. I study her a moment longer, ensuring she is still present and not locked in another nightmare. She's still with us.

A second later, my heart jumps up in my throat when I see the two most beautiful babies in the entire world. Although, I'm not sure they are actually babies. They look so grown already, but they are definitely Kai and Enzo's. They are a spitting image of the two of them.

Enzo walks over, holding the sleeping children. "Zeke, Siren, meet these rascals who have stolen our hearts. This is Ellie," he hands me the first child.

I'm holding Enzo and Kai's child. I don't think life gets any better than this. And just like that, I'm crying again.

"That's your Uncle Zeke, sweetheart. Don't tug on his hair even though he should cut it off," Enzo says.

"Don't you dare tell him to cut it off," Siren teases back.

I smile, brushing my hand over the little girl's hair. "You want to hold her?" I ask Siren, knowing Enzo wants to introduce me to his son as well, and I'm not sure I'm ready to hold two squirming kids at once.

Siren sits frozen for a moment, not answering. "Siren?"

After a beat, she extends her arms, and I give her the child. She holds her to her chest like a natural.

"And this bastard, is Finn," Enzo says.

"Language," Kai hisses, but smiles at me, as recognition hits my face.

"For Langston and me?"

Enzo nods and puts his son, who he named after me, in my hands. Finn is both my and Langston's middle name. More tears are fall. Langston should be here celebrating this moment with us. But that's not why I'm crying like a baby for the millionth time tonight.

I'm crying because I can't imagine a more perfect life. I don't know how they do it. Live in this world filled with danger and have the two most perfect angels in it with them. But they do. They are able to do both, and when I glance at Kai and Enzo, I know they are doing it without fear.

I glance over at Siren. She looks absolutely perfect, holding Ellie. I realize what I want. *This*—this is what I want. I want to be married to the woman I love, with as many kids as she wants, a job we both have a passion for, and good friends to share our lives with. *I want this.*

And I know who I want to share this life with, but I'm not sure Siren can be persuaded. I don't know if she wants to get married again. I don't know if she wants kids. I don't even know if she wants me.

But I have no doubt—this is what I want.

25

SIREN

WHEN I HOLD Ellie in my arms, I feel whole. I thought I was whole before, but I was wrong. This, holding a child you love, changes everything.

I thought I could be happy if I just had Zeke in my life. I thought our love was enough. I was wrong.

This is what I want—a family.

I want a marriage.

I want kids.

I want friends I consider family.

I want a life outside of killing, murdering, and stealing.

But I have no idea how to make that happen. None.

I can't see how Kai and Enzo make it work. They are obviously still involved in their criminal endeavors, but yet, they have two small kids. *Isn't that reckless? Isn't that asking for the kids to be stolen? To be kidnapped? To be hurt to get to their parents?*

If Julian knew about the kids, he would have used them instead of Zeke to get what he wanted. And I'm sure Bishop would do the same.

But damn does my heart open to the idea, the possibility, the temptation. I don't dare look over at Zeke while I'm holding Ellie. I don't want him to know what I'm thinking, what I'm wanting. We are so far away from being able to consider having kids that it hurts. I'm sure Kai and Enzo were responsible when they had kids. I'm sure they thought about everything. I'm sure they took every precaution.

I'm sure they didn't lie to each other. Betray each other. *Hurt each other.*

I'm sure they were always kind, loving, and honest.

I bounce Ellie on my lap. Think about something else. Think about the ocean. Think about the incredible yacht we are on. Think about how good the wine tastes.

But all I can do is look into the beautiful green eyes of this tiny girl. A girl who doesn't understand the dangers in her life she has because of her parents. A girl, who at such a young age, already has dreams and aspirations and goals. A girl who deserves the world. And if given the chance, will conquer it.

"Siren, you want to help me feed them and put them down?" Kai asks.

I nod, not realizing we've been playing with the kids for a couple of hours now. I've barely spoken a word, but I've felt Kai's eyes on me. I've felt her staring, but I have no idea what she's been thinking.

Kai takes Finn. I follow Kai into the yacht with Ellie in my arms. We head downstairs to a door. Kai enters a code and does a facial and fingerprint scan before the door opens. "You can never be too careful," Kai says bashfully as we walk into the children's nursery.

I smile. I would want at least that much to be able to sleep at night.

Kai hands me a prepared bottle, as I sit in one of the

rockers feeding Ellie. She feeds Finn his bottle, her eyes still lingering on me.

"Tell me what you're thinking. I know this is all a lot, and you're not as easy to read as Zeke is," Kai says.

I rock, looking down at Ellie before I clear my head and look at Kai. "What do you think Zeke is thinking? You know him well."

Kai smiles. "I do, and it's clear what that man is thinking. He's head over heels in love with you."

I exhale a breath preparing for my next question. "And what do you think about me? About our relationship? I mean, I don't think I'm right for him. I've hurt him too many times."

Kai laughs. "You're perfect for him because you think you're wrong for him. That means you want the best for him. And trust me, if you think Enzo and I's relationship was perfect, it wasn't. We've done things to each other you can't even imagine doing to Zeke."

"I've shot him," I say.

Kai's lips curl up. "I've shot Enzo."

I frown. "He bought me on an auction block."

"Enzo tried to sell me."

I take a deep breath. "I tricked Zeke into thinking I was on his side, while the whole time I was working for his enemy. Oh, and I was married to a man while with Zeke, and I didn't tell him."

Kai is quiet for a moment. Finn finishes his bottle, and she starts burping him. Ellie is still carefully working on her own bottle.

"We all do things in this world to survive. Stupid, dumb, horrible things. It doesn't mean you don't belong together. If everyone in this dark world were judged by everything they did, none of us would ever be worthy of a relationship. Don't judge yourself. Don't judge him. Somehow, you have both fallen in love. I can see why. But don't for a second think you don't deserve each other."

I swallow. "How do you do it?"

Kai knows what I'm asking. "I love Enzo. And I wanted babies. It wasn't planned. In fact, when I found out, I was scared to death. My life was extremely complicated at the time. When I had them, I thought they were going to be a blessing and a curse. But once they were here, I've never once thought of them as a curse. I have responsibilities to this company. I have men and women who count on me; I can't just quit my job. But I'm a mother and a wife first.

"Yes, I've brought them into a dangerous world. But in some ways, I think they are safer than most children. What other kids have a biometric security system, a yacht armed with enough weapons to take down a fleet of battleships, and a hundred men who would fight to the death to protect them? They will know what danger is and how to judge people before they turn five. They will know everything. There is nothing I will be able to hide from them.

"And if Enzo or I die protecting them, they will never have to wonder if they were loved, they will know. I can't think of a better way to raise a child."

I look down at Ellie, who is so content in my arms drinking her bottle. Her eyes are closed, and I think she's fallen asleep. She seems happy and loved and protected— everything a child needs.

Kai places Finn in his crib. And I place Ellie in hers. They are perfect.

Kai takes my hand. "Don't be afraid of your future. I know it seems bleak and scary right now because of the dangers you face, but I promise, it will be worth it. Zeke is worth it."

Zeke is worth it.

No, he's not. He's dangerous. He's going to hurt you. He's hiding things from you. You have to stop him. Get him to tell you the truth.

You're mine, not his. Mine, Bishop says.

No, get out of my head!

I will. When you do what I want.

What do you want?

"Siren! Siren, wake up! I'm here, I'm here," Zeke says, pulling me to his chest. As soon as he does, I'm pulled back to the world. He's my anchor to the real world. When he's holding me, he pushes Bishop out.

"Never leave," I cry into Zeke's chest.

"Never," he growls back, holding me tighter.

We sit on the floor, and it takes me a minute to register the babies crying and that I'm still in the nursery.

It takes me a few minutes more to return my breathing to normal, to calm down and be able to stand up. Kai and Enzo each have a child in their arms rocking them, trying to get them to settle down.

"I'm so sorry," I say when I stand, staring at the restless, crying kids.

"Don't be, it's not your fault. The kids are fine. Already going back to sleep," Enzo says. He looks from me to Zeke, giving him permission to take me somewhere calmer.

"Actually," Zeke rubs his neck. "I need to talk to Kai a minute."

Kai nods.

He leans down to me. "If I start you a bath while I talk to

her, will you be okay?"

I nod. "Yes." Although, I have no idea. I can't control my nightmares. I can't control who has control of my thoughts or voices in my head. I can't control anything anymore.

"Five minutes. I promise," Zeke says as he leads me to a bedroom and then into the bathroom.

"I can't believe there is a tub on a boat."

"Yea, Kai loves having a bath, so Enzo installed a bathtub in several of the bathrooms. And now that they have kids, it's necessary."

Zeke starts filling the tub with warm water. Then he kisses me tenderly before lifting my shirt up. He kisses my neck, over the curve of my breasts, and then down to my flat stomach.

"What are you doing?"

"Worshipping your body."

"I thought you were going to talk to Kai?"

"I am." Zeke kisses down my thigh as he strips off my jeans and panties. "But this way, I'll be thinking about you the whole time and hurry back."

I gasp when he kisses over my clit. His tongue stays in his mouth, but I feel just enough heat to turn me on and send chills up and down my body.

"Don't touch yourself while I'm gone," he says.

"Five minutes, and then all bets are off," I smirk as I climb into the tub.

He grins, watching me sink beneath the water. He kisses me on the forehead and is gone before either of us can change our minds. And then I'm alone.

"I can do this," I say out loud to myself. "One, two, three..." The only way I can force my mind on the moment is to count and focus on Zeke, so that's what I'll do until he returns.

26

ZEKE

LEAVING Siren alone kills me after she had another nightmare, but I need to talk to Kai. She needs to know all the facts to protect her family. And I need her help. I could ask Enzo, but Kai and I have a special connection. She will understand in a way that Enzo won't. Enzo will just want to protect his family, which I understand. But Kai has always considered me part of her family.

I find Kai leaning against the railing at the front of the boat, looking out at the dark sky.

I come up and stand next to her, not speaking. There is a shift in the air. A shift from the happiness we both felt before to a much more serious tone.

"When you were shot saving me, my heart broke. It was like nothing I've ever experienced before. Even thinking Enzo was dead didn't rattle me like losing you, Zeke. I can't explain our connection. It's different than any other in my life. It wrecked me. Maybe because you were the first person I ever truly loved that I lost. Maybe it's because you saved me by taking a bullet meant for me. Maybe we are really two halves of a soul."

"Stingray," I say, taking her hand.

Tears fall. Down her cheeks and mine.

"I'm not going to keep crying over you. I'm not going to feel guilty forever. I love you, Zeke. You know that. And when you died, a part of me died. I healed getting your letter that you were alive. I healed more seeing you alive in person at the ball. And seeing you now has done wonders to heal me. But you also hurt me by hiding. Promise me, never again?"

"Never again," I say.

She squeezes my hand.

"Now, tell me," she says.

I take a deep breath. "Siren has nightmares; she hears voices in her head, not voices...one man's voice—Bishop. He bought her. It's a long story that doesn't matter. But he had her, controlled her. We aren't even sure what he really did to her, but he fucked up her head. And now, at random times, she hears his voice. I've talked to doctors, but they say only time can heal her. That's not good enough. One man, Julian Reed, an enemy, says he can help her. But I don't know. I need help. I need to heal her. I'm scared for her. She can't keep living like this."

"We will do whatever we can to help you."

"Even give me a yacht?"

She laughs. "You can have all the yachts. Whatever you need."

"I'm not just here to talk about Siren."

"You're here to talk about Lucy and what you hid in my vault," Kai says, her lip twitching in anger.

"You're mad?"

"No, not really. I do wish you had told me. But that was before my time, so I understand why you didn't. Have you told Siren?"

My silence gives her her answer.

"You need to tell her the truth. I don't care about you hiding things from me, but if you love her, tell her the truth. About everything. Trust me."

"What does that mean?"

"Tell her everything you are feeling. Everything you want, as soon as you can. Don't wait. If you wait, it might be too late. There is only ever now in our world. Never a promise of tomorrow."

I nod, understanding. If I want to marry her, I need to tell her. Kids, tell her. A future, tell her.

"We will come up with a plan about the rest tomorrow, Zeke. I know you have a lot of enemies, but Bishop was on our radar before. And it sounds like Julian Reed is really after us, not you. We will fight them together. One by one. Just like we always do," Kai says.

"Thank you, but you need to know what I expect. I don't expect you or Enzo to put your life on the line, not when you have two young babies. Those babies will always come first. I will do everything I can to protect them above all else, I promise you," I say, looking her dead in the eye with the moonlight as my witness.

She frowns. "You can't promise me that. You have your own family to protect."

I've made promises to Lucy, to Siren, but this vow is just as important. I will keep my promises. To each of the women who are important in my life. I will protect them at all costs.

"I promise you, Kai. I'll keep you safe. I promise," I say again.

"You better," she says with a smile.

"I should get back to Siren."

"Go. Thankfully the rooms are soundproof. Have fun," she says with a wink.

Thank god for that.

I run back down the stairs, entering the code Kai gave me for the bedroom. Each room has top-level security. I can't think of a safer place than this yacht.

I walk through the bedroom and into the bathroom, where I find Siren, in the tub, touching herself.

"What. Did. I. Say?" I growl, my voice deep, dark, and scary even to myself.

Siren's hand freezes. Her eyes flutter up. Her eyelids are hooded. Her cheeks are shaded pink, and her lips are soft. Her legs are spread, and even though the soapy water blocks most of my view, my imagination and experience with her body fill in the rest.

"You going to join me?" Siren asks, her voice hopeful, not scared by my caveman-like voice earlier.

"I shouldn't."

"But you are," she smiles. She grabs my hand before I realize what she's doing, and yanks me down into the tub, clothes and all. I always forget that for such a tiny person, she has incredible physical strength. I've seen her do pushups. She has killer arms. I would love to workout with her and really understand the limits of her physical abilities. Although she's strong for such a tiny thing, her body is still small, and all muscles have limits.

I laugh, as water splashes out of the tub and soaks my clothes. "Did you miss me or something?"

"Or something. My hand wasn't doing as good of a job as your lips, tongue, or cock does."

"Oh, yea?" I ask, letting my finger fall between her naked thighs, teasing her entrance. I wish I could tell how wet she was, but her dark expression says it all—very wet.

I sit back on my feet and remove my wet shirt. She watches me with a thick intensity as she licks her lips and lets her hand fall back between her legs.

"No touching," I command.

She stops. "Then hurry. I need you."

Fuck, that voice. It does things to me. Drills deep into my core, telling me how much she wants me—no, needs me. If she only had a clue what that voice does to me. Her eyes fall to my crotch, where my erection is straining against my jeans, and I think she gets the idea.

I lean back and remove my shoes while she chews on her bottom lip, her breath speeding and cheeks flushing.

"You know I would have been faster if you hadn't had pulled me into the tub while I was still wearing clothes."

She moans. "Hurry."

I laugh and decide to take my time. I enjoy her watching me. And I enjoy having a perfect view of her body, while she has an obstructed one.

She arches her back and tosses her hair to one side in a fierce look. She leans close to me until our lips are inches from each other. "If you don't have your clothes off in the next five seconds and your cock slipping inside me a second after that, I'm going to come without you."

She falls back into the tub, her eyes full of her threat.

Damn.

I remove my pants and boxer briefs in record time, and then I'm pulling her on top of me, my cock resting at her entrance.

She grins.

"You know you shouldn't blackmail a man like that," I say.

"Mmm, I think I should, it seems to work," she shifts her hips and takes an inch of my cock inside her.

"You sure about that?" I slip a finger in her ass without warning as my cock drives inside her pussy.

Her nails dig into my shoulders as she moans, throwing her head back as the pleasure fills her body. "Ever had anyone inside this sweet ass?"

"No," she groans. "But now I want to."

I laugh. She's game for anything. I don't think she has sexual limits; she would try anything. Me slipping a finger in her ass barely even phases her.

Wheels turn in my head as I pump inside her with my cock and finger. "When we get out of the tub, this ass is all mine," I say into her ear before nibbling.

"God, why does that sound so incredible?"

"Because you love me and trust me to do anything in the world to your body."

"I do."

I glide her hips up and down over my cock, until both of us are in a delicious rhythm.

"We need to talk," I say suddenly.

She doesn't stop riding me. "Really? You want to talk now?"

"Yes," I breathe. Kai told me to tell her now. Not to wait. It feels like we should talk right the fuck now. I don't know why I feel so much urgency, but I do.

"We need to talk about our future. About marriage, and kids, and—"

Siren's head falls down, and she kisses me hard, her tongue pushing deep into my mouth, massaging my tongue and making me want to scream her name.

I forget about what I was going to say. Talking can wait. Kissing, fucking, and loving her cannot.

Our eyes lock open as she rides me and kisses me and

makes me forget about everything but her until our orgasms rip through us like a hurricane. Like a bomb going off.

She freezes.

"What?"

"Do you hear that?" she stops writhing and kissing me.

"Hear what?" But as I speak, I hear it. There are bombs and bullets ringing off. A sound we both know too well.

I push Siren off me in a flash, and we both throw on ripped clothes and grab our guns before running out of the bedroom, headed straight for the babies' room. There was no communication. No need to discuss where we are going and that we would both put our lives on the line to protect them.

We aren't the only ones who are running to the babies. Kai and Enzo are running, half-dressed and flushed just like us. Both wielding guns in their hands. All of us wearing a look of fear on our faces. But I feel guilt more than fear. *What did we do? What were we thinking bringing danger to their perfect life?*

27

SIREN

"Who's attacking?" Kai asks, looking at Zeke, then me.

Zeke frowns. "I'm not sure, but I'm about to find out."

"It's not Bishop," I say.

All eyes fall on me.

"I'd know. I'd feel him, trust me," I say.

"Okay, so that leaves Julian?" Kai asks.

I nod. I should know the most about Julian. I've worked for him for years, but I'm afraid I don't know him at all. "He's manipulative, but he has a lot of resources. If he attacks, it will be full force. But his goal is to manipulate and control."

Another round hits the yacht, and we all shudder at the sound as we stand outside the twin's bedroom. Enzo has the video camera pulled up on his phone. Somehow they are both sleeping silently inside.

"I've called for help, but the closest team is half an hour away," Enzo says.

Kai nods. For some reason, both men look to her to make a decision about how we are going to attack. She looks to her husband. "Stay with the kids. Protect them with your life. Don't let anyone into the room. No matter what. Promise me," she says firmly.

"But you should..." Enzo starts.

"You're a better fighter. They need you to protect them if we fail. Promise me, them first," Kai says.

"I promise," Enzo says with a frown. She gives him a quick kiss, and then he disappears into the room.

"The codes will no longer work. I can't even get into the room if I wanted to. It's bulletproof and bombproof. It would take sinking the ship to have a chance at getting access to the room," Kai says.

Zeke and I take a deep breath, knowing the babies are as safe as they can be.

"I don't think anyone knows you have kids," I say.

"Let's keep it that way," Kai answers.

"What's the plan?" Zeke asks, looking to Kai.

"We fight. Just like old times. We fight and hope we can outsmart a team of men who want to kill us. I'm going to head to the bridge to get this yacht moving as I'm the weakest fighter. You two do what you do best. Zeke, you are a master with a gun, and I have no doubt you are too Siren. Just cover us until I can get this yacht up to full speed. They won't be able to catch us then," Kai says.

We all nod as we head up the stairs.

I start heading to the right. Kai starts heading to the left to sneak up to the bridge.

Zeke stands in the middle, realizing he'll have to choose to go with Kai or me.

It should be an easy decision for him. I know who needs him more right now, but he stares at me like he can't bear to leave me.

I kiss him quickly. "Go, she needs your protection. If she doesn't get this yacht moving, we are all dead anyway."

He frowns, but I shove him toward Kai and head up the stairs before he has a chance to follow me.

My heart is racing harder than it ever has before, going into a mama bear protection mode over the two babies asleep downstairs oblivious to the dangers above. They aren't even my babies, but I feel the instinct. The intense desire to do whatever it takes to save them. Kai and Enzo must feel double what I feel. I don't care how many men are out here trying to attack us; we will kill them all before they even realize there are babies asleep downstairs.

I see a shadow moving. They are on the yacht.

Fuck.

I aim my gun and shoot at the end of the shadow, knowing I'm only hitting an arm at best, but it will be enough to disarm the person. I hear the grunt, and then I dash in clear view to finish him before they get a shot off.

The man falls to the floor.

Three men behind him fire at me in the dark. I hate the darkness. I wish I could say that I'm used to fighting in the dark, but I'm not. I'm a good fighter, but I'm better in the daylight when I can manipulate with my words and body.

I shoot quickly, sneaking around to the front of the yacht. I let my eyes lift enough to see over the railing, but not enough to get shot in the head.

Holy shit.

I see at least twenty ships. *Twenty.*

We're doomed.

There is no fucking way we can take down twenty ships full of men trying to kill us. There are just four of us. We can't hold them off for the thirty minutes we need until the rest of Kai and Enzo's team gets here. There is nowhere for our yacht to escape.

I feel us moving. Kai must have gotten to the bridge, but

we're barely creeping. There is no space for us to travel through.

Fuck.

I try to see who is in charge. *Julian or Bishop?*

Who do I want?

Julian.

Bishop scares the hell out of me.

But Julian has to die. We don't have a choice but to kill him, for so many reasons I'm still hiding from Zeke.

The boat stops completely a second later. I see more men on the boat. I kill them all one by one.

But then...

No!

I see a man holding a gun to Kai's head.

I see Zeke begging him to let her go. I see a dozen more guns aimed at Kai's head.

And then I see him—Julian Reed.

Of course, he's behind this.

You can end this, Bishop's voice says in my head.

I can, but not because Bishop wants me to. I want to.

I put my hands up and drop my gun, moving out of the shadows.

"Take me," I say, getting everyone's attention.

Zeke still has his gun pointed at Julian.

"Siren, what are you doing?" Zeke pleads me to stop, but he doesn't get a say. None of them do. If I can stop this, I will.

I turn to Julian. "Take me."

Julian grins. "Why my Aria, I'm glad you finally showed up. Thank you for leading me here."

"Liar. She didn't help you," Zeke shouts.

Kai tries to break free of the man who holds her.

Julian grins. "Fine, fine. You win. She didn't help me, but

she was easy enough to track when I have a tracker in her body. She makes it easy to follow."

Fuck, when did he put a tracker in me? And where?

I feel violated in a whole new way.

"Let her go. You want me, not her," I say.

"No, I want you all," Julian says, moving to stand in front of Kai and study her.

"I have Kai. My associate, Bishop, has Lucy—" Julian says.

"No," Zeke and I both say at the same time.

Julian turns to me. *He wants me.*

"Me for them," I say, knowing he won't take the offer, but I need to try.

Julian grabs Kai's hair roughly, pulling her neck back so she's forced to look at him. She stands strong. I know she wants to say horrible things to him, but she won't. She's a mom. She has to survive for her babies. She won't piss him off.

"Nope. Care to try again?" Julian asks, looking at me with a darkness I've never seen.

"Me to get you to leave. Take all of your men and leave. Me for not killing Kai, Lucy, or anyone else on this boat," I say, stepping closer.

"Siren, don't," Zeke says.

I glare at him, pleading him to stop. I don't have a choice. I have to do this, and he can't stop me. The pain in his eyes tells me he doesn't have another plan. He agrees, but he can't tell me to go—good thing he doesn't have to. I would give my life for these two women any day of the week. And definitely to save those babies.

"Do we have a deal?"

"Yes," Julian says.

I step forward carefully, but Zeke grabs me at the last

second. "Don't." I've never seen such pain. He's losing three women. All at once. He loves us all differently.

"I have to," I say slowly. "It will be okay. I'll protect them."

"I'm not worried about them. I know you'll protect them."

His eyes say he's worried about me.

"Come for us," I say, stepping out of Zeke's arms without a kiss, hug, or even an 'I love you.' If I did, I wouldn't be able to go. I walk over to Julian, trapped in his arms in an instant.

"It's nice to have you back where you belong, Aria," Julian says, kissing my hair, breathing me in, and dragging me toward his boat.

My eyes look at Zeke, who tries to chase after us. I shake my head. "Come for us. He wants to make a deal. It's all a game," I say, knowing Julian. *This is all a game to him.*

Then I say the thing that kills me. "Save them, not me. Promise."

Zeke doesn't promise. He doesn't say anything. He's just gone. I'm thrown into shackles, to be locked away with two other women Zeke loves. Women I promised I'd save no matter what.

I plan on keeping that promise.

28

ZEKE

I LOST.

I never lose.

We. Never. Lose.

Not like this. I've never lost a person I loved so much in this world. I was the one who was lost. I was the one who was killed. But them...they all survived. They all lived.

Today, that changed.

Julian has Kai and Siren.

And Bishop has Lucy.

I'm left heartbroken, with a hole in my heart the size of Texas. I failed—Lucy, Kai, Siren. I failed three women. I wasn't strong enough. I wasn't fast enough. I wasn't smart enough.

I let Julian Reed and Bishop outsmart me. I let them take people who were mine. They. Were. MINE.

Not anymore. Now, they are gone. Now, they are Julian and Bishop's. Now I have to fight to get them back, which is going to be harder than defending them in the first place. Now, I have to pray that nothing happens to them until I can get to them.

I have to leave right the fuck now. I can't give Julian more than a few minutes head start. I have to go. I have to save them.

Now.

But first, I have to do something just as difficult. I have to tell my best friend that I failed. I have to tell him that his wife is gone. That the mother of his children is gone. That this could be the end of the world as we know it.

He trusted me. And when it mattered, I couldn't protect them.

It feels a lot like last time. When I went into the ocean, I felt like a failure. Not because I was going to die, but because I wasn't sure that I had saved anyone. Although, this time, I know I failed everyone.

I walk down the stairs of the yacht, hearing a faint cry. Maybe it's my imagination. The rooms are soundproof, after all. The cry, fictional or real, breaks my heart all the same.

It's the cry of a baby who wants her mother.

I stand in front of the nursery door and knock. I'm not sure if Enzo can hear me or not.

"Is it safe?" he asks, through a speaker in the door.

"Yes," I answer back.

"What's the safeword?" Enzo asks.

"The what?"

"The safeword. Kai will tell you the word if it's really clear and safe. We didn't want someone to be able to be tortured into opening the door, so we came up with a safeword. Ask her what the word is. She'll have my balls if she finds out I opened the door without asking for the safeword first."

I grip my long locks in a fist, frustration, anger, and pain building and exploding through every pore in my body. I have to keep it together. I don't get to cry. I don't get to feel pain. Three women are depending on me. I have to save them. I have to protect them.

"Enzo, just open the door," I say.

"I can't. Where is Kai anyway?"

His voice is relaxed. He doesn't realize or even imagine that his wife could be gone.

No, she's not gone. Just missing—kidnapped. We can get her back.

"Enzo, please," my voice begs him to open the door. I can't explain to him what happened over an intercom. He needs to open the door.

Silence.

I think he's going to open the door, but he doesn't.

"Where is Kai? Where is stingray!"

Damn him for using the nickname I came up with for Kai. Damn him. The tears flow. The tears burn down my cheeks. I'm not going to survive this conversation.

"I failed. They're gone. All of them," I say, collapsing to my knees in front of the door like I'm asking for forgiveness, for mercy, but I deserve none. Especially not if Julian or Bishop lays a single finger on our girls.

Enzo doesn't respond. He doesn't answer at first. He waits.

Finally, the door opens. It shuts. It locks, keeping the twins safe inside.

"Get up," Enzo says, his voice low and deafening.

I stand, knowing what is coming, and I deserve it.

"Julian has Kai?" Enzo asks.

"Yes," I breathe, wishing I could take back the word. Saying it makes it true.

Enzo punches me. It's swift. It's efficient—a punishment for a crime. I failed him. I failed Kai, one woman I never thought I could fail. I deserve it.

I wait for a second punch. A third. A fourth.

But he doesn't punch me again.

I open my eyes. My face is spared more punches because he's a crying wreck on the floor in front of me.

"Did he take Siren too?" he asks. I sit next to him, leaning against the door with my own tears.

"Yes."

I expect another punch. Instead, he pulls me to him and hugs me. I hug him back. We sit like this for five long minutes. For five long minutes, we feel sorry for ourselves. We feel the pain, the fear. When our time is up, we abruptly stand up.

Enzo takes out his phone and makes a call.

I wait.

"Dammit, Langston, pick up your phone," Enzo yells into the phone. Then hangs up.

I frown. *Langston isn't coming.*

"You have to stay," I say, realizing our situation and hating it at the same time. It's why Enzo wanted Langston.

"Yes," Enzo breathes through his pain, cursing over and over again under his breath.

Enzo picks up his phone again. "I'll call Beckett. He can help you."

I nod. If Enzo trusts him, I trust him. Enzo makes the call.

"He'll meet you in St. Kitts in an hour."

I nod as my life flashes before my eyes.

I should have married Siren when I had the chance. I should have made her mine. I should have had babies and found us a deserted island away from all of this.

I should have killed Julian. I should have spent my time tracking Bishop and killing him, not trying to get closer to Siren by sharing my past with Lucy.

I should have told Siren every truth.

No—I shouldn't have. Not knowing the truth could save her.

"Zeke, you got this. Go get them back. Give them whatever they want. Money, power, everything. Do whatever it takes to get them back. Do you hear me?" Enzo says.

He grips my shoulders, staring at me with everything he has—all his pain on full display. I hear the babies crying, and his head turns. He left the monitor on. I see a man being torn in half—wanting to save his wife, but needing to protect his kids.

"Take whatever crew you need. Do whatever it takes, but bring them back," Enzo says.

"I will," I promise. I will. I have to. It's the one promise I will keep.

29

SIREN

My head bobbles back and forth as the plane shifts in the air. My arms are tied behind my back; my ankles are tied up as well. My head is groggy after being drugged.

I could get out of the bindings in about five seconds. *But then what?* I'm thousands of feet up in the air. I can't fly a plane. I'm stuck until we land.

I look over at Kai, who is lying against the wall of the plane, still out of it from the injections they gave us. The drugs left my system hours ago, but her smaller frame takes longer to expel them from her system.

I watch her sleep. She looks peaceful, but a drug-filled sleep is anything but. It's deep, dark, and heavy. It pulls you under, playing with your mind until you can't think about anything other than wanting to escape. But you can't escape. The drugs have a hold of everything.

Kai's body twitches—she's coming out of it.

I pull my hand free of the bindings so I can stroke her back as she wakes up.

"Hey, I got you. Take a deep breath," I say, patting her back as Kai wakes up.

She sits up suddenly, rocketing from asleep to wide awake in seconds.

"What happened?" Kai asks.

I frown. "Julian Reed has us on a plane. He's kidnapping us and using us to get whatever is in your vault that belongs to Lucy, Zeke's old girlfriend."

Kai shakes her head, trying to clear her head. Then she nods in understanding. "I remember."

I bite my lip. Not remembering isn't good, but sometimes remembering can be even more torturous.

"Here, let me get those off you," I say, quietly, eyeing the closest guard who appears asleep in his chair a few rows in front of us. We're in the back of the plane, on the floor, hidden from view of most of the men.

I untie Kai's hands, and then we both untie our legs before leaning back against the wall. We enjoy feeling a little freer now that are hands and legs aren't tied up.

"Did Zeke tell you what's in the vault?" Kai whispers.

"No."

Kai frowns.

"Are you going to tell me?"

"I don't know. I want to protect you. And I don't know if you knowing is going to protect you or make you vulnerable."

I sigh.

"Ultimately, I need to honor what Zeke wanted, which was for you not to know. That's his way of protecting you."

I nod.

"Zeke will come. He'll fight. He'll rescue us," Kai says.

"So will Enzo."

"No, he has to stay with the twins. We made a promise to always put the twins first."

I swallow down the lump in my throat. If it comes down

to it, Zeke better choose to save Kai, not me. I don't have little lives depending on me like Kai does. The world is better off if I'm dead. If I survive this, the wrath I'm going to bring down on this world has never been seen before.

"So, what's the plan?" Kai asks, her eyebrows raised.

"What? You mean you don't want to wait for Zeke or the guys to come save us?" I ask with a small smirk on my lips.

"Hell no."

"Have I mentioned how much I like you?" I ask.

She grins.

We take a few minutes to study our surroundings, to form a plan. There is a room at the front of the plane that I'm sure Julian is in. Then there are a few rows of guards in the seats near us. Then us at the back, given as much attention as cargo. They think we are tied up, drugged, helpless women. *They are wrong.*

"How confident are you with a gun or knife?" I ask Kai.

She takes a deep breath. "I'm better with a gun than a knife. Zeke helped teach me how to shoot. But I saw you on the yacht. You are way better at both than me."

I squeeze her hand. "If Zeke taught you how to shoot, then I trust your skills are above average."

"I'm so happy he found a woman like you."

"You mean a woman who gets kidnapped and brings him danger all the time? You sure he shouldn't have settled down with a nurse or teacher or something?"

Kai laughs quietly. "You're the woman for him."

"Thanks."

"Now, let's figure out a plan."

We formulate a plan, a plan that involves us attacking during landing.

We see land out the window quickly approaching. That's our cue.

I wink at Kai. *Sure, Zeke is a great partner to take down a plane with, but I suspect I'm going to enjoy working with Kai a lot.*

I creep forward on the plane, holding the rope used to tie up our arms and legs. They thought they could use it to bind us, but I'm about to use it to kill them all.

I reach the first man, a drunk playing games on his phone. *What an idiot to underestimate us.*

I throw the rope around his neck and pull hard, while Kai covers his mouth to keep him silent while he dies. The man struggles and succeeds in pushing Kai off him, but I hold tight. He makes a small gargled sound. I watch as one of the guards starts to turn around, but Kai already has a gun. She fires, hitting the man square in the head. Turning to the last guard, she shoots him square in the chest.

I blink rapidly. "I'd say you are better than above average. You can fight with me any damn day of the week."

I toss the rope to the floor, next to the body of the man I just strangled to death.

Kai's eyes widen. "Remind me not to get on your bad side." She looks down at the dead man.

I crack my neck as I walk up the aisle and grab one of the guard's gun.

That was the easy part. The hard part is going to be killing Julian, who most likely saw us kill his men on a security camera.

I move my hand to the doorknob.

"Come in, ladies. I've been expecting you," Julian says from inside before I open the door.

I frown at Kai, who looks worried. The lines around her eyes have deepened, and her jaw is tense.

We've come this far. We aren't just going to surrender. Not without a fight.

I open the door and step inside, my body blocking Julian's view of Kai.

But Kai doesn't want me to protect her. She steps inside the room right after me, and we both aim our gun at the man sitting at a table with a whiskey and a cigar.

He has five guards with guns aimed at us.

Julian looks at his watch. "I'm impressed. You took out three men while you were unarmed and still feeling the effects of drugs in under three minutes. Impressive."

I growl.

"Please, sit. You must be famished," Julian waves to the table in front of him where there is enough food to feed a dozen people.

"We aren't hungry. We're here for one reason."

"To kill me. Yes, I've heard that before. How many times have you or Zeke tried to kill me and failed?"

I frown. *Too many.*

"You forget why I know you won't kill me. You know the consequences if you are the one to kill me. And I'm not sure she is capable of killing me," Julian looks to Kai.

"I can kill you as easily as Siren can," Kai says.

Julian shakes his head.

"Try." He motions for his men to put their guns down. They do.

I glare at Julian, knowing this game too well.

Kai fires.

Julian ducks, and then fires back.

"No!" I scream, running to Kai.

"I'm fine, I'm fine," Kai says, her voice breathy from being shot in the arm.

"You didn't have to do that," I say.

Julian shrugs. "She shouldn't have missed."

I hold Kai as we collapse to the ground. I take off my

shirt and tie it around her arm, ignoring the heated stare I'm getting from every man in the room. *Thank god I wore a bra.*

"What do you want, Julian? Why are we here?" I ask, knowing he'll answer. He always does.

"I want what's in the Black vault," Julian says, looking at Kai. She doesn't blink as she glares back with steely resolve.

"I need Lucy to be able to open it, once I have it," Julian says, looking off into the distance. *That's why he needs Kai and Lucy.*

"Why me?" I ask. He doesn't need me. He knows I know nothing about what's in the vault.

"Because I want you," Julian says. He's always wanted me. I don't have to ask what for. I'm done talking to him.

I hold Kai until we land in St. Kitts. I'm handcuffed, dragged off the plane, and loaded into a van next to Kai. The men are gentler with Kai.

"I'm fine, stop looking at me like that," Kai says.

"I'm sorry. We shouldn't have done that," I say.

"Yes, we should have. We got answers. We are one step closer to getting free," Kai says.

I nod. *She's right. We can do this. We can free ourselves.*

But when we are dragged to a dungeon on Julian's property, and I see Lucy in the cell—dirty, pale, and trembling—I'm scared.

It's all on me.

Kai is injured.

Lucy is dying.

I'm the only one strong enough to protect us. Kai can't because she has her kids to think about. Lucy can't; she can barely breathe, let alone hold a weapon.

It's all on me.

Zeke, hurry your ass up.

30

ZEKE

I STARE at the compound that is Julian's house, Beckett standing next to me.

"Wait. The plan is to just ring the doorbell?" Beckett asks. He's already heard the plan, but he thinks I'm crazy. Luckily, he's not in charge. Enzo and I are. And Enzo is good with my plan.

"Yes," Enzo and I say for the hundredth time. I say it in person, while Enzo says it from an undisclosed location where he's watching the twins and monitoring us through body cameras and earpiece radios.

Beckett sighs, running his one hand through his hair. He's a good man, but he's not Langston. Beckett cares about Kai; he's here for her. He and Enzo are brothers, so Enzo trusts Beckett with his life. Therefore, I do, but it's not the same.

We don't have enough time to wait for Langston to come back from off the grid. I'll deal with that asshole later.

"Let's go," I say, stepping forward. Beckett walks with me. The house is also surrounded by a dozen of Enzo's best men, ready to move in as soon as the civil negotiations end.

"Don't fuck up," Enzo says from the earpiece in my ear.

"Shut up, dipshit; you aren't helping," Beckett says, patting me on the back.

Neither of them is helping.

I ring the doorbell and wait.

Two seconds later, the door opens. It's opened by an armed guard, instead of one of Julian's house servants.

"Right this way," the man says, eyeing us both. He doesn't pat us down. He doesn't ask for our guns.

Somehow that feels worse. It means Julian is so sure we won't use them that he isn't even going to bother taking our guns from us.

We are led into a large room in the basement. Julian is waiting in the center of the room, and a dozen guards line the walls.

"Thank you for coming," Julian says. "Would you like a drink?"

"We aren't here to drink. Where are they?" I ask.

"I think we will all have a drink first." Julian snaps his fingers, and a man pours three drinks, setting them all at a circular table in the center of the room.

"Only three? Bishop isn't joining us?" I ask. Beckett and I reluctantly sit at the table.

"No, he had other business to attend to," Julian answers.

Fuck.

"Fuck," Enzo says in my head. "He's going after the vault, thinking we are all distracted with saving the girls. I have men protecting the vault, but my best men are there. It won't be enough."

Unless Kai already had the item they want moved. I wouldn't put her past her. She's smart. She knew the value of it. She knew the vault wouldn't hold it forever.

I ignore the bourbon poured for me. I reach into my

pocket and slide the keys to the yacht across the table. "The yacht you requested."

Julian grins, staring at the keys. "I would say nice work, but that was the easiest task I've given you yet."

"Don't play games, the only reason you gave me that task was so you could track me and get the girls," I say.

Julian looks from me to Beckett. "Don't act like you really care about them. You would have brought more than a one-armed man with you to save them if you did."

Beckett and I both move to kill him, but Enzo shouts in our ear, "Don't fall for it. He just wants you to show your cards. Let him know how many people you brought with you. Don't fall for it."

I grab Beckett's arm, keeping him seated.

"Let's finish this truth or sins game. I'll tell you whatever you want. I'll answer your last two questions. Then we can be done with this," I say.

Julian takes a long puff on his cigar, blowing smoke in our faces.

"I don't need you to answer any questions. I have three women who are more than capable of answering questions," Julian says smugly.

A door opens behind him at his words, and I see them.

Lucy.

Kai.

Siren.

My heart beats faster and slower at the same time, seeing them all alive. I study each closely, though.

My heart stops looking at Lucy. I'm terrified for her.

Lucy looks horrible. She's whiter than a ghost, her bluish hair has faded, just like the life that has clearly seeped out of her. *What did he do to her? What torture did she suffer?* She's barely hanging onto life.

My heart skips a beat looking at Kai. I'm pissed.

Her arm is bleeding, and a shirt is tied around it, keeping the blood from spilling out. She looks strong, fierce, unbreakable. But beneath her armor, she's terrified she won't make it back to her family.

My heart races, looking at Siren.

Siren is the only one unhurt physically. She's standing in her jeans and sports bra, her hair tied back in one of my scrunchies. She looks like a warrior princess. I have no doubt her wheels are turning, figuring out how to kill every man who dares to touch her or her friends.

I let out a breath. *They are all still alive.* That's what I have to focus on.

"They're fine, chill," Julian says, sipping his drink while watching me.

"Lucy sure as hell isn't fine! Kai is bleeding! And Siren—"

"Siren is the only one you care about, and I haven't touched her," Julian says.

I growl. "I care about them all." I stand up, slamming my hands down on the table. I want to kick some ass, but I have to wait. I could take down every man in this room, but there are three women who could get seriously hurt if I'm not careful.

Beckett takes my arm and sits me back down.

"We will give you whatever you want. Do whatever you want. Just let them go," I say.

"I know, but you fascinate me, Zeke. You have since the moment I met you. Since you took Siren back even after she showed her loyalty was to me. I have what I need. You and I should part ways today. I don't need you to complete two more rounds of our game. But..." Julian takes a drink, pausing for dramatics.

"But Bishop isn't done with you. So I have to keep you around. I'll give you something in good faith."

"What do you mean?"

"You just completed a task. That earned you your choice of women, but only one."

I frown.

"Fine, then tell me the other two tasks now, and I can take all three with me."

"No, you get one. You get to save one. After I decide on your next task, you'll have a chance to save another. Although, I can't guarantee the state she will be in when I return her to you."

My hands ball into fists, and then I'm reaching for my gun. I just can't with this asshole anymore.

"You won't complete the final task I have planned for you, so the third woman—she'll be mine forever," Julian says.

I aim my gun at Julian's temple at the same time Beckett does.

"Give me all three, now," I say.

Then I notice the guns aimed at every woman's head. None of them tremble. None of them show weakness. All would die for me. And none of them would haunt me for eternity for letting them die.

"Choose. Which woman will you save? From torture, from suffering."

"You already hurt Lucy and Kai! I can't save them from all the pain."

"Lucy arrived in this state. Pretty sure she's sick and dying. You might want to save her, if you want her to live." Julian stands, walking over to Lucy, brushing his hand through her hair.

She doesn't fight him. That's not the Lucy I know. The

Lucy I know, would have punched him. *How did I not see this before?* She's dying. I have to save her.

Julian walks over the Kai, who stands taller, not looking at me or him. If Kai looks at me, she knows I'll see the pain at not being with her kids. She knows I'll choose her. And she doesn't want me to.

"Are you going to choose this exotic creature? She must have a story and a history with you that I'm just itching to learn about. I would enjoy breaking her spirit."

"Don't touch me," Kai growls at him. He stops, loving her feisty reaction.

It makes me sick watching him touch her and imagining what he would do if I left her, if I couldn't save her. He would rape her, break her, maybe even kill her to get information from her.

"Don't worry, the bullet wound is just a surface scratch. You should teach her to aim to kill, though, so this doesn't happen again," Julian teases.

I frown, not wanting to know what happened to earn her that wound.

And then Julian moves to the woman I'm dreading looking at because I know what I'll find.

"Or will it be Siren, my Aria, here. She's everything you could want in a woman—strong, beautiful, can fire a gun better than most men. You're clearly in love with her. But is she in love with you? That's the question. Has she been tricking you this entire time? Is she still loyal to me? Would she be worth saving?"

Julian doesn't touch her. He knows he'll end up with a fat lip if he does. Siren has the most bindings on her—handcuffs around her wrists and ankles. Heavy chains constrain her while the others are just tied with rope. She broke free before in their presence. She can save herself. *But can I stand to leave her behind?*

"Choose one to save—one to leave with you. We can meet back here in a week to discuss your fourth task. And if you complete it, that task will earn the freedom of one more woman."

A week is too long for him to have two of these women. I can't leave any of them here that long. But I can take one now. I can save one now without a fight. As soon as that person is free, then I can fight to save the other two.

Choose.

I can't choose. I love all of them.

"Zeke," Siren calls to me.

Don't look in her eyes. Don't...

But, of course, I do. She's already made the choice. She knows who I should save. And it's going to kill me to do it.

31

SIREN

SEE, the bastard isn't even going to save you. He's going to choose to save someone else. He doesn't love you, Bishop's voice floods my head.

No, focus on Zeke. Let him be my anchor.

I push Bishop out. I won't let him back in. Not right now. Not when I need to help Zeke choose. I need to give him all my strength. *I can do this, I won't break.*

"Choose. Who will it be?" Julian asks, loving this moment—his sick, twisted game.

Julian and Bishop are just alike. They both like playing games, playing with people's minds. No wonder they work together.

I can't talk. Julian won't allow me, but I hold Zeke's gaze and tell him everything I can.

Lucy is dying. I should have told you, but she wouldn't let me. I've got her. I'll stay with her. I'll comfort her. She doesn't want to be saved.

Zeke looks at Lucy with a broken heart. Lucy nods and smiles at him, ready to die on her own terms.

Zeke swallows his pain and looks back at me.

Kai has two babies who depend on her. You know she's the choice. She's the only choice.

I'm strong enough to survive until you get back. Take Kai. Save her. Then come back to me. I won't let Julian or Bishop or any man touch me, I promise.

Zeke reaches into his pocket. Julian doesn't notice, he's too amused with the game he's devised to destroy the man I love.

Julian thinks he can destroy love.

He can, comes Bishop's voice. *Love doesn't exist.*

I grin.

Love does exist. Love can't be destroyed—not ever. Not a love like ours. Not a love like Enzo and Kai's. Not a love like Lucy's.

Zeke walks over to Lucy and whispers something in her ear. She smiles at him.

He walks over to Kai and looks her dead in the eye, a silent conversation passing between them. She shakes her head.

Then Zeke walks to me and presses something into the palm of my hand.

A ring.

I don't look down at it. I don't want Julian to see and take it away from me.

"Marry me?" Zeke whispers into my ear and steps back.

My heart flutters for an entirely different reason. For hope. For a future. For love.

I have something, someone to live for. I have someone who is going to love me forever. I'm not going to let Julian or Bishop take that from me.

"Yes," I breathe back with the biggest smile I've ever had on my face as I look at Zeke.

He grins back, his smile just as bright. For a second, I

know that everything is going to be okay. Someday, we are going to live together. Someday, we might have kids and a beautiful house where we grow old together. *Someday...*

Julian looks at us. "So, I'm guessing you choose Siren?"

Zeke takes another second to look at me.

I nod my encouragement. *I've got this.*

Finally, Zeke looks at Julian, knowing he can't look at me when he speaks his decision. "I choose Kai."

32

ZEKE

SIREN SAID yes to marrying me. *She said yes!*

That's what I focus on as I lead Kai out of Julian's house. I focus on the small victory. I focus on the fact that it will only be minutes before getting to fight for Siren. *What can Julian do to her in minutes?*

Nothing.

But Lucy, god, Lucy...

Siren will protect her until I can get to her. Then I'll take her straight to a doctor.

As soon as we step out of the house, Kai punches me in the shoulder.

"Why did you save me?" Kai yells. She turns to Beckett. "And why did you let him?"

Beckett frowns, pulls out his phone, displaying a picture of the twins. "They are why we saved you—*them*. Don't you dare make us feel bad for choosing you."

"She's safe?" Enzo's voice breaks in my ear.

I pull out my earpiece and give it to Kai. "Talk to your husband. Then tell me we shouldn't have saved you."

Kai takes it. "Siren's strong. Stronger than me and more skilled. She'll be okay."

I nod. "I know she will. But Lucy..."

Kai rests her hand on my shoulder with a frown. "Even if you had chosen her, I don't think you could have saved her. Siren will be with her."

"I should be," I say.

"Then get your ass back in there and save her."

I look at Beckett. "Get Kai somewhere safe."

He nods. "Be careful. Julian's going to be prepared for you to attack. And we have no idea where Bishop is." Enzo said he never showed up at the vault.

I look at Kai, who just winks at me, telling me she moved the item they are all fighting for. I would trade it away in a second if it would free Siren and Lucy. But apparently, Julian and Bishop would rather play games.

Fine, I'll finish the game by killing them all.

I take the earpiece back from Kai. "Get ready to attack on my cue," speaking to the men surrounding the house, waiting to attack.

"Go get your girl," Kai says.

"I asked her to marry me," I say.

She laughs. "Of course, you did. Good, we can have a big double wedding when this is all over."

"I thought you were already married?"

"I am, but I want a big wedding where we can celebrate with all of our friends."

I grin. "Double wedding it is."

"Where am I taking Kai?" Beckett asks.

"Airport. You remember, Nora? She'll get you to Enzo," I say.

Beckett stills at her name, but nods. I'm not sure if he's happy or scared to be seeing Nora again.

I ignore him. Whatever drama is going on between the two of them can wait until later.

I check that all my guns are loaded. "Let's go," I say, giving my men the signal to move in.

With my size sixteen boot, I break down the front door. No one greets me this time. It's eerily silent.

I hear several of my men give all clears as they enter the house.

Hmm, strange. "Head to the basement, that's where I left them."

I open the basement door and head down the stairs first.

At the bottom of the stairs, nothing.

It's a ghost town.

Like moments ago didn't even happen. It was all a dream.

"Search everywhere," I command as men file down into the basement after me.

"Clear."

"Clear."

"Clear."

Each time a man says that, I become more afraid. *How the hell did they get out of here so fast?*

Where are they?

"Over here," one man says.

I run over to him.

"There is a tunnel," he starts.

"Fuck," I say.

"Through the tunnel, everyone," I say. *I'm coming Siren, just hold on.*

I jump into the dark tunnel first and start running, not waiting for my men to follow.

Suddenly, I hear the explosion.

I turn and run but get hit by a falling rock anyway. The

tunnel is closed off as I stare up from where I am on the ground, pinned under a large boulder.

"Well, that couldn't have worked out better if I had planned it that way," a woman giggles. "Oh wait, I did plan that."

I stare into the darkness, trying to spot from whom the voice is coming, but I can't see anything but shadows in the dark.

"Who are you? What do you want?" I ask as I struggle to get free. I don't have my gun. It lays a few feet in front of me. I dropped it when the boulder hit me. The rest of my weapons are pinned under the boulder.

Fuck.

The woman leans down, out of the shadows, until I see her face.

"I'm your worst nightmare," she says.

In that moment, I realize I'm not going to be keeping my word. I'm not going to be able to keep my promise to Lucy or Siren. I'm not going to save them. They are on their own. It's going to be a struggle to even save myself. A struggle to even keep my promise to marry Siren someday.

33

SIREN

WE'VE BEEN MOVED three times. Three different countries. Three different planes.

I hold Lucy to my chest as she coughs. I suspect it's pneumonia. Her body is weak; she can barely breathe. She has breast cancer, but right now, it's not the cancer that's going to kill her. It's the infection, the cold, the pain.

I hold the ring Zeke gave me in my hand, refusing to put it on. He should be the one who does that.

But I read the engraving over and over.

I promise...forever.

"He's not coming. He's going to break his promise," Lucy says.

I frown. "Zeke's coming."

Lucy shakes her head. "It's been three days."

"We've been moved all of those days. It takes a lot of effort to track people all over the world. He's coming."

"No, he's not. You have to save yourself, Siren. Save yourself."

"Stop. He's coming. And I'm here to protect you. You just focus on staying alive."

"I'm dying. There is no reason to save me. They can torture me, and I won't tell them about the weapon."

"Weapon?"

"Yea, my big secret. You should know."

"No, Zeke didn't want me to know." He thought it could save me. If I know, they can torture me. They can torture me now, and I won't be able to help them because I don't know the truth.

Lucy raises her eyebrows, reading my mind.

"My mom, she was a genius. A crazy, psychotic woman, but also a scientific genius."

Even if they torture this secret out of me later, I'm not stopping a dying woman's last words.

"She was always in the lab. Always studying. Determined. She was a horrible mother. Never around to watch out for me. But a genius in that lab."

Lucy takes a deep breath, her voice weak, her body trembling from the cold. I squeeze her closer to me, begging her to continue.

"One day, she discovered how to create the ultimate weapon. Guaranteed to kill any man..."

"What did she discover?" I ask, my voice weak.

"The cure."

I frown. That doesn't sound like a weapon.

"The cure for cancer."

"Lucy, that's a cure, not a weapon."

Lucy shakes her head. "No, she discovered how to help people live, but also how to infect people with a vicious form of cancer. A contagious cancer. One that can spread."

"But she discovered a cure. Why didn't you take it?"

Lucy looks up at me. "Because no one should live forever."

"But it wouldn't be forever. It would have given you a full-length life."

"Yes, but it would have destroyed everyone. I'm the only one who can open the container. The cure and the curse, the cancer that could be used as the ultimate weapon. This is my destiny. To die. To let the weapon die with me."

"Oh, Lucy. You're the bravest, strongest woman I know." I stroke her hair, holding her chilled body tighter in my arms.

She smiles. "I'm pretty badass, aren't I?" coughing her words.

Her suffering kills me.

"What can I do?"

"I want to see the stars one last time."

We are locked in an underground dungeon with bars and keys and locks.

"Okay, I can do that. Julian!" I shout.

It takes a minute, but it gets his attention via a guard.

And then he's standing at the door, watching me.

He smirks. "Yes?"

"Give us five minutes outside, alone."

"And why would I do that?"

"I'll give you what you want."

"Which is what?" Bishop enters the basement, crossing his arms.

Both of them in the same room scares the shit out of me.

"Lucy told me how to access the weapon. I'll tell you whatever you need to know. I'll even give you myself to own, just let us outside," I lie.

Lucy coughs.

"Who are you promising that to? We can't both control you," Bishop asks.

Julian rolls his eyes. "We are on the same side. Does it matter?"

Bishop leans forward. "Yes, it does."

"You two can decide who gets to control me later. Do we have a deal?"

The men exchange glances, then Bishop nods. Apparently, he's the one in charge, which terrifies me.

Julian and I already have an agreement, an understanding. He knows I won't break my promise, and I know he won't either. But Bishop, I have no idea.

Julian unlocks the door. "Five minutes. If you run..."

"She's dying. I won't leave her," I say angrily.

I lift Lucy up and carry her up the stairs. I don't know where we are, but it's somewhere warm, I realize when I stand outside. I make my way over to a patch of grass overlooking a small pond. I lay Lucy in my lap, looking at the water.

The sky is clear, the stars and moon shining down on us.

"Here we go, Lucy. The stars are beautiful, aren't they?"

She nods.

For a moment, we are just two women, who have been lucky enough to be loved and be in love, looking up at the sky.

"Can you do something for me?" Lucy asks.

"Anything," I say, trying to hold back my tears as I hold her.

"Tell Palmer I loved her. She was the love of my life. Not Zeke. She's mad I chose death over our love. Tell her I love her. It was always her. And if could, I would have lived forever for her."

I can't hold back the tears now. They stream down my cheeks.

"I promise," I say.

I hold Lucy against my chest.

Bishop and Julian argue behind us about who will.

control me. The consensus is that Julian can have his way with me first, but Bishop will be the one to break me. Bishop thinks he already has control over my mind.

I know what my fate is. Zeke can't save me. He broke his promise to come back to me, although I'm scared to know why.

I won't be able to save myself either.

I look down at Lucy, making the ultimate sacrifice. She's giving up her love—her life. To protect us all from something her mother created.

I don't care what those men do to me. All I care about is this—being here for an amazing woman and letting her love flow through me. I don't care about Zeke's promise. I care about Lucy's.

As I watch Lucy leave this world peacefully, with love in her heart, I realize love is the only thing that can save me. It saved Lucy from living in pain.

I hope love is enough to save me from the pain I'm about to endure...

The End

Thank you so much for reading! Zeke and Siren's story continues in Fallen Love

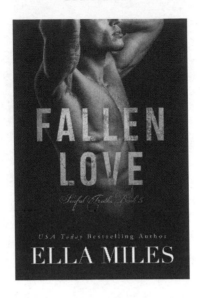

Grab the entire Sinful Truths series below!
Sinful Truth #1
Twisted Vow #2
Reckless Fall #3
Tangled Promise #4
Fallen Love #5
Broken Anchor #6

Read Enzo and Kai's story below in the Truth or Lies series!
(You also get to read Zeke's beginning)
Taken by Lies #1
Betrayed by Truths #2
Trapped by Lies #3
Stolen by Truths #4
Possessed by Lies #5
Consumed by Truths #6

FREE BOOKS

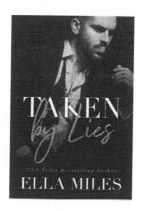

Read **Taken by Lies** for **FREE**! And sign up to get my latest releases, updates, and more goodies here→EllaMiles.com/freebooks

Follow me on **BookBub** to get notified of my new releases and recommendations here→Follow on BookBub Here

Join **Ella's Bellas FB group** to get **Pretend I'm Yours** for **FREE**→Join Ella's Bellas Here

ORDER SIGNED PAPERBACKS

I love putting my signed paperbacks on SALE!

Check them out by visiting my website:
https://ellamiles.com/signed-paperbacks

ALSO BY ELLA MILES

SINFUL TRUTHS:

Sinful Truth #1

Twisted Vow #2

Reckless Fall #3

Tangled Promise #4

Fallen Love #5

Broken Anchor #6

TRUTH OR LIES:

Taken by Lies #1

Betrayed by Truths #2

Trapped by Lies #3

Stolen by Truths #4

Possessed by Lies #5

Consumed by Truths #6

DIRTY SERIES:

Dirty Beginning

Dirty Obsession

Dirty Addiction

Dirty Revenge

Dirty: The Complete Series

ALIGNED SERIES:

Aligned: Volume 1 (Free Series Starter)

Aligned: Volume 2

Aligned: Volume 3

Aligned: Volume 4

Aligned: The Complete Series Boxset

UNFORGIVABLE SERIES:

Heart of a Thief

Heart of a Liar

Heart of a Prick

Unforgivable: The Complete Series Boxset

MAYBE, DEFINITELY SERIES:

Maybe Yes

Maybe Never

Maybe Always

Definitely Yes

Definitely No

Definitely Forever

STANDALONES:

Pretend I'm Yours

Finding Perfect

Savage Love

Too Much

Not Sorry

ABOUT THE AUTHOR

Ella Miles writes steamy romance, including everything from dark suspense romance that will leave you on the edge of your seat to contemporary romance that will leave you laughing out loud or crying. Most importantly, she wants you to feel everything her characters feel as you read.

Ella is currently living her own happily ever after near the Rocky Mountains with her high school sweetheart husband. Her heart is also taken by her goofy five year old black lab who is scared of everything, including her own shadow.

Ella is a USA Today Bestselling Author & Top 50 Bestselling Author.

Stalk Ella at:
www.ellamiles.com
ella@ellamiles.com

Made in the USA
Columbia, SC
25 July 2022